THE
JOURN
HUMPHREY ILKES

Also available from Book Guild Publishing
by the same author:

Non-fiction

The British Hearse and the British Funeral
(fully illustrated)

Railway Fiction

Murder on the Santa Special
Trackbed Tales

Sherlock Holmes series

The Missing Earl
A Case at Christmas
The Russian Connection
Disquiet at Albany
To a Country House Darkly

THE AMAZING JOURNEY OF HUMPHREY WILKES

N.M. Scott

Being the altogether fictitious account of the recovery of an Edwardian bicyclist knocked down by a motor-omnibus in Cambridge in 1913

Book Guild Publishing

First published in Great Britain in 2015 by
The Book Guild Ltd
9 Priory Business Park
Wistow Road
Kibworth
Leics LE8 0RX

All characters in this publication are fictitious and any resemblance to real people, alive or dead, is purely coincidental.

Typesetting in Garamond by
Keyboard Services, Luton, Bedfordshire

Printed and bound in Great Britain by
CPI Group (UK) Ltd, Croydon, CR0 4YY

A catalogue record for this book is available from
The British Library

ISBN 978 1 910508 70 1

For Julie and Bill, Ben and
Annika and Justin (and baby Penelope)

Acknowledgements

A big big thank you as always to all the team at Book Guild Publishing. Thanks also to the ever-dependable Amanda Payne and Sylvia Bedford.

My name is Humphrey Wilkes. I am a research scientist at the university, and it was upon one chill, autumnal morning towards the end of October 1913 that I happened to crash my touring bicycle in Cambridge, sustaining a badly fractured skull.

I was hospitalised for some months, undergoing various operations involving fearful hand-drills and serrated saws and, while in a state of coma – I must emphasise this, on the borderline between life and death – a most unusual occurrence took place. For, while my body remained prone and very still, my poor old head bandaged more tightly than any Egyptian mummy, it appeared my imagination took flight, my mind became overactive and I was spirited upon a journey, an amazing adventure so vivid and real, I might as well have been living it.

Prior to my unfortunate collision in which my Townsend Tourer and myself were crushed beneath the front wheel of a motor-omnibus in South Street, I was planning a short holiday with Thompson and Mr Clancy and Lucy Eldridge and some of the other ladies from my Cambridge faculty to the village of Karstein in the German principality of Volknik, some thousand miles or so from Leipzig.

In order to prolong my life, of which the surgeons were

to a man despairing, and held little hope of saving, I was apparently encased in ice for the sake of my damaged skull, for the duration of an exploratory operation. My core body temperature was thus reduced drastically and Professor Sir Alan Canty, himself a Cambridge man from the Institute of Neurology, thereafter began a surgery, which I was later informed was both frighteningly innovative and unprecedented, for doctors had already determined splinters from my perforated skull had pierced the soft tissue of the brain and such a dire prognosis offered only a one-in-a-hundred chance of survival.

* * *

'Gentlemen, I shall do all in my power to stabilise the patient's vital organs, but I would concur with the anaesthetist that the inherent shock to the system from the removal of the top of the skull by means of a surgical saw and our former procedure of hand-drilling through bone will have taken their toll upon the central nerves and put incalculable strain upon the heart's ventricle chamber.'

* * *

There was a wintry nip to the air. It had been snowing when I found myself walking down the garden path to a familiar scrolled, wrought-iron gate at the far end, flanked on either side by a clay brick wall. I was at home in Cambridge. I was wearing a pair of sensible brown brogues, my usual bowler, a gabardine coat with my pipe and tobacco pouch in the pocket, and brandishing a furled umbrella, one of a stock with bamboo handles I normally kept by the hallstand and useful for rainy days.

An iron gate opened onto a little patch of turfed ground where some pumpkins grew wild. There was a potting shed, outside which my gardener kept his wheelbarrow, and a handy cart made from a rusty old perambulator, and an oak barrel water butt beside the shed. I unclasped the latch, aware of the usual squeak of rusty, unoiled hinges and the clang of the sprung gate as it closed behind me. I stepped forward and where there should have been solid ground, instead I instantly sank down, plunged knee deep into a drift. My entire perception underwent a devastating change, for the landscape before me had altered wonderfully – an unending vista of white, a plateau of ice and snow stretching as far as the eye could see – a vast canopy of dark sky, a barren land certainly, and intensely cold.

My clothing, although ideal for Cambridge when cycling home of a damp winter's afternoon when gas lamps are lit early, I found hopelessly inadequate for trekking in sub-zero temperatures. The biting winds of the plateau caused such searing pain to my temples as cannot adequately be described. My brain felt as though it were expanding inside my skull and solidifying into a frozen lump.

If at this, the first phase of my journey, there were any tests of endurance to pass, I failed on every count. I had quickly been reduced in a matter of hours from human to automaton. No inward reserves of strength did I possess, no great courage, no mental stamina, no apparent goal, save to plod wearily through the snow, one foot in front of the other – a vague, impulsive inner drive to move, to advance. And then somewhere in the distance, where there was a range of mountains, I heard a loud and booming train whistle. I stopped in my tracks, keenly listening, all my senses alert, but the whole process of listening so intently utterly exhausted me and, hearing no more of the train, I was about to collapse in a frozen heap, give up and lie down, let the snow completely engulf and cover me up, obliterate my mind, my personality and my aching body. My core body temperature at this point was very low, dangerously so, in fact, when… Ouch! I had come up flat against something hard, stumbled blindly into an obstruction of some kind, a monstrously large obstruction at that. Not glacial but metallic. Scratching at the layer of ice formed on my spectacles, as my vision gradually focused my breath was taken away by the wonderment of it all, for through the falling snow I gazed incredulously at the front end of a locomotive. The engine was green and sported a very fine brass-rimmed chimney and brass dome.

'I'm hopelessly lost,' I called out to no one in particular, my clothes stiff as a board from accumulated ice, so weary was I that I cared not unduly when the locomotive talked back.

'Well, you'se bloomin' well on my passenger list,' said a metallic, cockney-sounding voice. 'It's Mr Wilkes, ain't it, from Cambridge? The wagon-lit coach will h'i trust meet with your approval. All is prepared, your compartment is laid out for dinner and, after your five-course meal, pyjamas, cologne, fragrant soaps and a shaving kit are ready for your personal use.

'I h'am to be your guide, on the first leg of your journey that eventually takes you south to Karstein in the principality of Volknik.'

'Why, of course, Karstein is my holiday destination.'

'This is the Great Northern Railway, sir.'

'I see, well thank you. Your name, if I might enquire?'

'Hadley Grange, sir.'

'Well, Hadley, I am very glad to make your acquaintance.'

Once I had clambered on board and found myself in

a luxurious wagon-lit compartment, I heard the engine blowing off steam and, after a noisy blast of whistle, a steady chuff-chuffing developed and the train started to build up momentum and we headed off across the great plateau shrouded by darkness.

After my meal, served via the dumb waiter, I took a long, soapy bath and, after changing into my pyjamas and dressing gown, plumped myself down on the compartment seat by the window. I peered out and all was very wintry and icebound. The plateau appeared to be undergoing an endless winter's night that stretched interminably.

A stranger tapped at my compartment door, passing along the corridor no doubt. Someone must have noticed even through blinds that my lights were on and decided to seek out some company. The door slid slightly ajar.

'Good evening, sir, may I eh…?' The fellow carried under his arm a bulb-handled cane.

'Of course,' said I, lighting my pipe and relaxing, but then something strange occurred. The train compartment of the wagon-lit, as warm and cosy an environment as any, well-heated and comfortable, began to alter. A hoar frost slowly began to encroach upon everything. First the compartment window iced over from the inside, the wire racks and lampshades upon their appointed brackets froze up and dripped a pelmet of icicles. The walls soon iced over and forming on the upholstery was a rime of frost both white and sparkling.

I observed with some amusement that my pipe was frozen solid and the very soles of my slippered feet now stuck fast to the floor, as though glued down. I myself had become frozen to my seat, but not through fear, say by being confronted by a ghastly apparition, but rather simply from the abrupt dip in temperature, for the plump gentleman sitting opposite wearing a shovel hat, naval coat, white breeches and worn buckled shoes was of a genial and pleasing disposition. He slumped back with a sigh, before apologetically explaining the phenomenon we were presently undergoing.

'Forgive me, bringing along my chilly ambience. I inhabit the ice plain out here on the plateau and rarely get a chance to come inside in the warm. My natural environment is many Celsius below – I live out on the frozen plateau.'

'You are not Jack Frost, at any rate,' I laughed.

'No sir, I am Sir John Franklin at your service. May I enquire where on the Great Northern Line you are headed? Hadley didn't say.'

'I am holidaying in Karstein in the principality of Volknik.'

'Oh, down south. I didn't realise, you're not like me, an intrepid explorer then.'

'Are you *the* Sir John Franklin of *Terror* and *Erebus* fame? Why, that is extraordinary. Your last expedition was in 1845, surely?'

'Indeed, I never got back to England, unfortunately, but we won't dwell overly on that side of things. What I really wanted to tell you is by way of a friendly warning between two English travellers in foreign climes. Be always extremely wary of whom you meet up here – apart from me, of course. Be damn careful, sir, your life may depend upon it.'

'Humphrey Wilkes. I am a microscopic scientist from Cambridge.' I leant over and we shook hands. I quickly withdrew for I felt my core body temperature plummet and the tips of my fingers burn terribly. 'Pray, could you be a little more specific?'

'Wilkes, I shall be frank. Your journey across the plateau

must necessarily be an arduous one. Once you have quit the relative comforts of the train your life will be fraught with danger at every turn. Hadley, charming though he is, represents but a short interlude.'

'I understand.'

'No, you do not, young man. Those that lurk up here will seek to snuff you out, lure you to your doom.'

'Listen, Sir John, I am perfectly capable of fathoming the gist of your warning, and I, a mere scientist from Cambridge, am both honoured and privileged that a great explorer such as yourself shows so much concern on my behalf. You refer to beasts such as the polar bear that roam these parts in search of their next meal?'

'Bears, what care I for they? Bears are rarely seen in these parts. No, I refer to another species entirely. I like you, Wilkes, a scientist to boot! I shall do my damnedest to make sure you come to no harm. What you will face out here goes against all logical reasoning, sir. Nothing can prepare you for whom, or rather what, you will encounter.'

I began to feel the drip of water upon my forehead, a dribble running down my nose. Sir John reacted swiftly.

'Ah, a sign. Well, sir, I shall be on my way. It has been a pleasure to meet you, Mr Wilkes. I trust we shall meet again next time, in much worse and more uncomfortable circumstances, I fear. Goodnight, rest in your bunk awhile. You will need all your strength; every atom of your constitution shall be tested to the limit.'

With these telling words my illustrious companion raised his shovel hat and passed into the corridor, sliding the door shut behind him.

My wagon-lit compartment instantly returned to being warm and commodious, my pipe re-lit itself and smoked the same as before, as though nothing had happened, the chilly atmosphere having retreated from whence it came. I stretched out my legs and considered all that Sir John had intoned, smoking all the while, gazing out of the window reflectively as the train rattled onwards.

* * *

I had hardly finished eating my breakfast when I sensed a change. The beat of the locomotive had altered, the steady, regular chuff-chuffing slowing down until I heard the steam engine apply brakes and, by the lurching of the table contents, understood we had reached an abrupt standstill. After a period of sustained high-speed running, powering across the great plateau, the train was now at a bare station halt in the middle of nowhere. A ferocious snowstorm was blowing and it looked very cold and uninviting out there. But Sir John's words that Hadley 'represents only a short interlude' came back to forcibly remind me that to continue my journey to Karstein I would now be once more facing the elements.

'This is where you get orf, sir. Keep walkin' in a due northerly direction for a mile or two and you'll come to a tourist office. I'll no doubt be seeing you again when you return to Cambridge after your 'oliday.'

'Thank you so much, Hadley. It's been a pleasure to travel with you.' I gathered my bowler hat and furled umbrella from the rack, and stepped down from the wagon-lit carriage, facing the ferocious biting wind with a dejected grimace.

At this juncture, more than ever it dawned upon me that I was not part of an official team, an advance party of men, a determined group of comrades set upon a planned expeditionary goal, but, rather, a solitary individual, alone and bewildered, crossing this vast continent of ice and snow, hoping for the best. Still I progressed somehow, doggedly plodding, forcing one foot in front of the other, trusting my instincts, gritting my teeth, until lo and behold, I saw with some relief up ahead that there was what I presumed was the tourist office – a rough wooden hut lit from within by a lamp. The wind had died down and the ice storm had become more intermittent. A shabby fellow smoking a pipe, wearing a fur parka, a hood draped over his head, approached through the snow.

'What do you want, old boy?' he barked out.

'I am Humphrey Wilkes, a microscopic scientist from Cambridge. I am journeying to Volknik.'

'Captain Scott, glad to make your acquaintance. The weather is somewhat inclement but that is to be expected at this time of year.'

I understood this chap to be *dead* along with his expedition party, and was surprised, to put it mildly, to be presently talking to the ghostly embodiment of the former explorer, a hero in England, certainly. My journey through the frozen wastes was already proving sufficiently intriguing.

'I am, sir, anxious to reach the village of Karstein. It lies in a small principality further south, so I am assured.'

'Karstein – the Castle Vratnik. I have heard mention of it certainly. Look here, old man, you look all in, in no fit state to make a long journey. We ourselves have not eaten, nor enjoyed proper sustenance for some time and you are very welcome to share a supper, stay the night, take a warm bunk by the stove, for I observe you are overly chill and sweated. Oates can rustle you up one of his pemmican concoctions. There are plenty of chocolate rations and tobacco. You must build up your strength. Karstein is many miles due south.'

The need for warmth, human companionship and shelter overtook me and I at once complied. The explorer took me by the arm and led me inside the dimly lit, wood-slatted hut.

The men were seated around a deal table, graced with an oil lantern effusing a queer, dingy glow, sewing and mending fur boots. The soaking snow, the need to surmount ridges of sastrugi, wore at the bindings and soles dreadfully as I myself could attest, looking at the sorry state of my own hopelessly inadequate footwear.

'Your ship, the *Terra Nova*, waits in the Sound,' said I, determined to test them out, and reaffirm a sense of reality. 'You must be anxious to meet up with your compatriots and make steam passage for England.'

'The ship left long ago,' sighed the tall and lanky fellow wearing a roll-neck jersey, frayed at the sleeves. 'And we find ourselves hopelessly adrift.'

'But the expedition hut remains.'

'Indeed. My name is Evans,' said another fellow, offering me his cold, clammy hand.

'Drat it, sir,' insisted Oates. 'You need *fattening up*. I shall boil some pemmican on the stove. We have a stock of canned eatables, dried biscuits and so on, enough nutrients and proteins to bolster your meagre diet. The loss of body fat remains a problem out here, if you are man-hauling sledges over long distances, as we have done, exposed to the ice storms upon the shelf.'

I confess the singular way in which the group of men regarded me caused grave concern. The members of the Scott expedition appeared to be pining fervently for something as yet unresolved. They, to a man, seemed singularly uninterested in the pemmican boiling in the saucepan. All eyes were upon me! And this presented me with something of a dilemma. The waxen, pinched faces, hungry and uncertain, hairy with interminable growths of beard, the violet-rimmed fishmonger slab eyes, the repeated repulsive lizard-like licking of chafed and wounded lips, warned me intuitively to be extremely wary of my companions in that isolated hut.

'*Fattening up*' – a reference to beef cattle, else livestock surely. Of course, I recalled from newspaper accounts that Captain Oates was responsible for caring for the ponies, the animals on the ill-fated expedition only a year earlier. I deliberately tested once more the reality of my sojourn in this region of intense cold and desolation. These men were, after all, my fellow countrymen. We were geographically linked. Our temperament and education should have been similar.

'The pit ponies are hardy four-legged omnivores. Do you feed them hay? How do such beasts of burden take to this frozen wasteland?' I asked, taking out my pipe.

'Eaten and digested thoroughly by carnivores. We are all of us now, I fear, of a predatory disposition, Mr Wilkes.'

Predatory – the word and the way he said it troubled me greatly. Here was I, invited to share a meal, I had been offered lodgings for the night, a warm bunk to sleep in and yet... A horrified feeling akin to revulsion swept over me, as I realised I was the only living being amongst a group of dead, stranded souls who appeared to me to be overly concerned for my continued sustenance.

One of my most telling observations concerned the iron stove, in fact unlit, cold and brittle and yet there seemed to be adequate warmth and the temperature of the hut felt passably comfortable. *Get out, get out, get out* was my innermost compulsion. For God's sake, the pemmican was boiling, steaming in a saucepan, but how? *Get out, get out, get out* – things are not quite as they should be.

'I shall not detain you further, gentlemen,' said I on a freak impulse. 'I am extremely grateful, Captain Scott, but I would not dream of imposing upon your hospitality. The hut's food store must be a most precious, yet limited, commodity. One more mouth to feed would be intolerable.'

'No, no, my man. You misunderstand,' insisted the explorer, desperation evident in the higher velocity of his speech. 'Stay, old fellow, my men can kit you out in some decent fur skins, boots, a parka, dry underclothes. That city bowler, gabardine coat and your brown brogues are hopelessly out of place in this hostile, freezing environment. Stay, I say, just for the night. You are most welcome at our hearth. Fill your pouch with tobacco and enjoy a pipe and a glass of whisky.'

How glittery and feverishly excited did the captain's rheumy, fishmonger slab eyes appear by the lamplight. However, a somewhat awkward attempt at a smile unmasked the pretence. A merely forgetful gesture concerning his briefly parted lips revealed to me the true horror of my predicament. Gracious, the over prominent canines, the ghastly white fangs that spoke to me of life's blood draining away.

I confess I flew from that place as fast as my wretched plodding footsteps through layers of snow would allow, determined to risk frostbite, even death, at the jaws of the freezing plateau rather than the fate that would surely be mine should I have delayed at that cursed hut for five minutes longer.

I trudged wearily across the frozen plain, the distant lamp-lit wood hut of Scott's soon concealed by a drift, the wind chill had if anything increased. My gaberdine coat, bowler and Oxford brogues were hopelessly inadequate for this kind of trekking, and I wished I had at least managed to purloin a decent set of furs back at the hut's expedition stores. How much further? 'Where, for God's sake, am I headed anyhow?' I wondered out loud. North – where the devil's north?

'Karstein,' a friendly voice intoned. Long, bony fingers bit into my arm and pressed. 'Have a care, sir, you are headed in the wrong direction. I shall set you to rights. The principality of Volknik lies some considerable distance further south.'

'I am indebted to you, sir, for your timely assistance.'

'Sir John Franklin at your service.'

I was struck by Sir John's distinctive double-breasted high-collared naval tunic, his chubby, genial countenance apparently impervious to extreme temperatures of cold adorned by an Admiralty hat. Incredible to think this man, this guardian figure of mine who appeared to have adopted my interests out here, had fought at Trafalgar. Also round his neck he wore a most large and impressive medal that I was later to learn was an award of the Knight Commander of the Royal Hanoverian Guelphic Order presented to him by his king.

'Why, what a joy and privilege to meet you again,' said I. 'Are all of you famous explorers set here for eternity? Would you be good enough to draw back your upper lip, Sir John? Merely as a precaution. I've just had a rather close call with Captain Scott and his party.'

'Certainly,' he answered, giving me an enquiring glance. 'I myself remain uninfected. However, I regret to say that Francis Crozier, the captain of one of the vessels provided by the Admiralty for my memorable if ill-fated 1845 expedition to search out the Northwest Passage, is most assuredly a practising vampire, as, alas my dear Wilkes, are a fair percentage of the one hundred and thirty-nine officers and ratings once placed under my command who crewed the two ships *Terror* and *Erebus*.'

'I shall make it my priority to avoid each one of them – ah, a set of perfectly preserved lead dentures, copper wired. I am relieved to see your canines are extinct but an awareness of the poisonous proclivities of lead is of course some way in the future.'

'You bamboozle me, Wilkes. Lead is a pliable and useful metal. Dear me, but Crozier, he is a slippery eel of a fellow, be sure to stay clear of him and the rest. You must always be watchful for prey seekers, Mr Wilkes.'

'I shall bear all that you say in mind, Sir John. My bearings out here on the plateau are, I fear, haphazard. I am a city man used to my comforts, entirely unused, and I might say, unsuited to this lengthy and perilous journey south on foot to locate the principality of Volknik.'

'Now, Mr Wilkes, pay close heed. You observe that heap of drifting snow up ahead where I am pointing my cane?'

'I do indeed, Sir John.'

'Well, climb to its summit and that, sir, is it.'

'Is what?'

'The travel office. Sir John Franklin at your service,' said he with a low bow, and with those words he vanished into the snow, merging with the wind-blown ice crystals.

I was by now feeling the full effect of my considerable excursions since leaving Scott's hut, and very tired and weary of the same white expanse of ice and snow before and around me everywhere. Using all my remaining strength, I staggered up a drift, and taking the route Sir John had earlier indicated, flecks of snow blew about, settling on my gaberdine coat and icicle-encrusted bowler.

There appeared over the ice ridge a timber-roofed building advertised as a tourist office and I confess in my state of exhaustion I imagined nothing could surprise me in this place any more, but something did manage to surprise me and I say, most devastatingly. A firm tap upon my shoulder and the resulting horrifying face I encountered when twisting round nearly caused me a heart failure; the shock of actually seeing my assailant sent me in terror of my life.

'You're that damned fellow Crozier. Sir John warned me our paths might cross,' I cried, brandishing my upraised brolly uselessly.

Attired in an unkempt nautical uniform of navy blue with faded gold epaulettes, white breeches and rotten buckled shoes, the man before me possessed a mauvish demeanour, reminiscent of overly long hung game. The glassy, waxy condition of stiffened facial sinews and flesh would, I am certain, accompany those buried and unfetchingly preserved in shallow graves under snow and ice for long periods. But here, not properly fettered as a good Christian surely should be, a mouthful of gleaming fangs grinned back at me, betraying his particular allegiance.

Before I could but step aside, the fiend had pounced on me and we fell and tumbled amongst the powdery snow, where Crozier pinned me down and fed hungrily. I felt a terrible rending of the cords of my neck muscles and two sharp stings before I fell into a void of deepest red.

* * *

Hospital Report

'Blood, dammit, Sir Canty, he is losing blood – we have successfully removed the offending splinters from the frontal

lobe and now this. The patient is haemorrhaging. We shall require pints and pints of blood to be transfused if we are to stabilise him. Hurry, nurse, for God's sake apply the transfusion needle to the vein in his stomach. Time is of the essence if we are to save his life.'

* * *

I could but vaguely discern the pale and translucent features of a beautiful woman leaning over me. Her hair was centre parted and straight and long, tumbling over her elegant shoulders. Her lips were vividly ruby red and trembling.

With her pincer-sharp fangs exposed, the lady had opened a gash in her slim, feminine wrist and bid me drink.

'Here, sir, sup your fill. That's it, clamp your weakened jaw upon my wrist and bite hard. Do not be fearful, I am strong among women. You must re-energise yourself and quickly. It was fortunate I happened to be roaming in this desolate region. I have encountered your kind before, or at least the steaming fleshy heaps, the fatty remains, carcases of lost explorers spread over the ice floe after a polar bear had eaten his fill.'

'Explorer? I am no explorer,' said I, my greedy mouth smothered in her rich, sweet-tasting blood, already feeling its revitalising effect upon my weakened constitution. 'I am a microchemist from a Cambridge faculty. Humphrey Wilkes.'

'Hush, Mr Wilkes, continue enjoying refreshment, drink for a while. See, my cleansing, redeeming blood flows abundantly. You shall soon be feeling gorged and replete, properly sated and your old self once more.'

'Crozier,' I gasped, suddenly recalling the fearful encounter in which I was grappled to the ground and severely bitten upon my neck. 'He gorged upon my life-force. He may yet be close by, madam, and preparing to pounce – even upon you, my pretty, divine angel of the cold northern climes, for your charismatic and healthy countenance so developed and womanly may yet attract a wolf still hungry for more.'

'Put your mind at rest, Mr Wilkes. I and my sisters are well able to deal with the proclivities of these unrestful souls, your captain is but an impertinent whippet. Indeed, his one hundred and thirty-nine stranded shipmates are now severely depleted.'

'From lead poisoning, else the polar beasts that roam the ice plain. Is that what you infer? I asked, sincerely.

'By us, my dear Mr Wilkes – by us *women of the twilight.* There, rest awhile, I say. I promise you shall come to no harm. Perhaps I can assist you to your destination – which is?'

'Karstein.'

'In the principality of Volknik. Yes, of course, I know Castle Vratnik, certainly.'

'May I enquire your name, dear lady?'

'Lucy – Lucy Eldridge.'

Lucy Eldridge – but I knew that name, it struck a chord, a distant resonance in my memory – whatever – at that stage I was still regaining strength and far too muddled to dwell upon the implications. I turned instead to consider my future holiday arrangements.

'Karstein.' I spoke the name wistfully, recalling my holiday destination fondly. 'Bradshaw's *Continental Guide* gives it the thumbs up – "A region in the principality of Volknik and herein resides a most picturesque and traditional forest village."'

'Very pretty and autumnal at this time of year, famed

for its jack o' lanterns, it's essentially pumpkin growing country.'

'Yes, I think Bradshaw's refers to something about pumpkins.'

'To reach Karstein you must head much further south,' directed my pretty vampire friend. 'The only known transport going that way is a cab.'

'A cab, you say. God bless petrol and a set of four sturdy wheels encased in pneumatic tyres, a motor taxi should be most agreeable. Why, I could while away the time in both warmth and comfort, a cabby doing all the driving.'

'A hansom cab I refer to, Mr Wilkes,' Lucy corrected as we clambered up the slippery slope towards the travel office. She held me in a tight grip, for since Crozier's ambush I was still weak on my legs. 'Drawn by a horse. You will be able to catch a connecting train once you reach the forest, I promise.'

'But a horse, for goodness' sake, will take forever.' I was frankly appalled. 'A lifetime surely, and I mean to say, Lucy, where's the road? Out here in the plateau there's not even a muddy track fit for a horse to travel along at two miles an hour.'

'Trust me, Humphrey, there is a way across the mountain range. Don't look so down in the dumps.'

That blasted travel office was no more than a shanty, corrugated roof, a stove-pipe chimney that hadn't seen a puff of smoke in years. I saw no indication of life or business activity whatsoever. Three snowy steps led up to a shabby-looking door, which at least I was pleased to see had a prominent 'OPEN' sign dangling on it.

Once we had struck a match and lit the oil lamp hooked from the ceiling, we were able to see better. There was little office furniture save a long, low, cushioned seat, a wall clock unwound and missing the hour hand, a counter with no documentation, pamphlets or travel brochures, and a solitary pot-belly stove, long extinct of heat, secured in a corner.

One item did stick out prominently, however; a large tourist poster showing a field of cultivated pumpkins, rows upon rows of them, and proclaiming in big capital letters: 'VOLKNIK – THE LAND OF THE GOURD.'

Wearing her tightly fitting frock coat and mauve ankle boots, Lucy strode purposefully across the bare floorboards and gave the reception bell a hearty slap. No one answered its pinging summons and the travel office I took to be deserted and wholly void of any living thing, apart from us. I suspected I must have been the first tourist to have called here in a very, very long time. I gave a nervous cough and, shivering with cold, moseyed into the centre of the hut.

'It's no use, Lucy, I'll never get to Karstein at this rate,' I sighed, fingering the newly formed scab on my neck, which was itching intolerably. I looked once more at that travel poster. *Pumpkins.* Funny, I seemed to recall there were some wild pumpkins growing at the back of my garden in Cambridge, round by the shed.

Lucy bent forward and spoke directly into my ear. 'Your outlook is a trifle pessimistic, so closed to cosmic influence. I rang the reception bell, did I not? Now, tell me please what is it you hear, yes? Listen, concentrate.'

The clip-clopping of horses' hooves bearing round the corner. I was frankly astounded. I sat on the low, cushioned seat and listened, and then I watched through the window as a hansom drew up outside the ramshackle tourist office. A gorgeous chestnut mare trotted to a standstill and obediently waited by the entrance. I observed its glossy flanks steaming and could only admire such noble deportment in a horse.

'But there's no driver,' I exclaimed, hardly believing what I saw. 'No cabman in charge of the reins.'

'Cannot a horse, such an intelligent beast, be capable of making its own decisions without a master's whip to scold? Hélène, my beauty,' Lucy cooed. 'Volknik, do you know of it?'

The horse whinnied, flicking its silken mane, the muscles and sinew of its powerful forelegs tightening and flexing in anticipation.

'Will you take Mr Wilkes to the forest region by the southerly route…?'

The chestnut mare began nodding and scraping its hoof in the snow. The cab shifted on the axle of its two gigantic wheels, so eager was she to get started.

'….keeping clear of Captain Crozier and his men?' The horse neighed, snorting smokey vapour.

'The deal's done,' said Lucy, helping me heave myself off the seat and guiding me swiftly outside. 'Hélène was once ill-treated by a member of Crozier's crew, who tried to corral her. She hates them nearly as much as we do. She thinks them uncouth and dirty, don't you, dearest? The lead contaminating their beings gives her the collywobbles.'

The vampire, who obviously shared an affinity with animals, stroked the mare's muzzle, as if by magic producing a rosy red apple which she fed the horse.

'Step in and I'll shut the front up,' she said at length, sensing I was growing jealous for attention. 'There, Humphrey, let me straighten your bowler for you. That's it, button your winter overcoat tight. Now, settle back and I'll heap these tartan blankets about your person. You're exhausted. A good, long rest is what you need most – yes? The journey to Volknik will take several days at least.'

Lucy threw in my bamboo-handled umbrella, tucking the blankets around my knees. I was vaguely aware of her leaning over, not kissing me exactly but rather nuzzling her sharp fangs affectionately against my cheek. Presumably this was my vampire's way of showing intimacy, of sealing a friendship, and I liked it very much.

'Oh, do keep tickling me with your fangs, Lucy,' I sighed, pleasantly content with my lot and glad to be on my way at last to Karstein after so much delay on the great plateau.

'It's a lot warmer down south,' I heard my angel Lucy say as the chestnut mare trotted off and the next phase of my journey began.

Before I fell into a deep and untroubled sleep, I honestly wondered if Lucy might care to accompany me on my journey south to this land of the pumpkins, a foolish notion I realise, for although we took pleasure in each other's company, the gulf between our species was far too great and her need to be once more amongst her own kind predominant.

* * *

At some juncture upon my journey across the mountains to Volknik, my slumber was disturbed by the surprise arrival of a fellow passenger to share my cab, an intrepid fellow who wore his by now familiar shovel hat, torn-about naval tunic and white breeches and buckled shoes. Unknown to me, he had been tapping away at my skull with his bulb-handled cane, getting little response.

'Awake, are you, Wilkes?'

I noticed the inside of the hansom was given a coat of hoar frost, my posterior glued to the seat by encroaching ice and the flip-up window, crisply covered with a thick rime of frost, entirely crystallised but from the inside outwards. Sir John Franklin remained himself unaffected by his chilly ambience and was puffing upon a churchwarden pipe. Hélène, the independently minded chestnut mare, a distorted wobbly countenance, trotted along regardless.

'Look, for God's sake!' he cried, his face turning grey, holding a silver hand mirror up to my face, my mouth gaping open like a gormless carp, for I had suffered a blocked-up nose and been breathing in this way. I peered dozily into the glass reflection and blanched.

'My teeth, dear Lord, how can this be?' I yelled, shocked out of my mind. The silver mirror, however, did not deceive. I was showing the beginnings of a growth of sharp pointy fangs. The evidence was stark and unequivocal.

'Think back, my lad. I am well versed in vampire law, particularly in more frozen climes. Your cause be not yet a lost one. You do not as yet lust for blood.'

'Certainly not! Is it Crozier's doing?'

'Hogwash! We already know about him, vile, coarse and leaden to the extreme. Lucy would have adequately rid your blood of his impurities when she allowed you a transfusion from her slender wrist.'

'Lucy? Well, now you come to mention it, Sir John, you know back at the travel office, shortly before my departure, she did sort of nuzzle my neck with her fangs. But I don't think she bit me.'

'Oh, what a fool you are, Wilkes, to be so unguarded. Compose yourself, sir, this instant and allow me to carry out an examination. Ah, no fresh bruising do I see, nor any vein punctured. Had she supped, your metabolism should have been done for and you doomed to "turn".'

Sir John hastily rearranged my shirt collar and I was

pleased his amiable, bewigged countenance was restored, his eyes appraising me, full of friendship and affection.

'Why sir, your neck and cheeks be merely lightly grazed, you appear untouched and we must be grateful for this. Any female vampire should find your physique irresistible. The blood pulsing through your veins and arteries I refer to of course, Wilkes, not your manliness.'

'Tell me truthfully, Sir John, is there still a risk I might turn?'

'Bless you, no, you are but blood-linked to Lucy. I suppose over time you shall become more and more infatuated – in love with her – if you will. I cannot speak plainer.'

'Well,' said I, somewhat relieved, 'that cannot be a bad thing, surely.'

'How I despair of these female vampires. Lucy, Sharna, Griselda and the rest. They be tricky wenches for sure, warrior females and such mercurial creatures. Despite promises, they more often deceive, be quite charming and life affirming one minute, then sup on you at the drop of a hat.'

'Blood-linked, you say.'

'Indeed, your long-term prognosis be favourable. You shall soon return to normal. Lucy, I venture to say chose to establish a blood-link between you and her. This be crucial for she shall in future be able at any moment to sense your predicament, whether good or ill, on the plateau. The better if you should come to grief. A navigational tool similar to my compass or, say, the modern sextant I became well acquainted with.'

'But that's amazing.'

'Impressive, certainly. Their brains be far advanced to your own, Wilkes. Why sir, to their kind you are but a backward species, a dunderheaded loon. I grant a vampire warrior is a splendid ally, though for Lucy to have chosen to take you under her wing baffles me.'

'Tell me, Sir John, are these women the most powerful vampires out here on the plateau? She seemed to me more than a match for Crozier.'

'Nay, t'is the elderly, the old timers, those that were here long before the *Terror* and *Erebus* expedition. Vitus Bering and Chirakov be the most feared and powerful of them all. They were the first vampires to migrate north and form a colony.'

Using the tip of my tongue, I searched carefully along my top row of teeth. The lengthening of the canines appeared only temporary and the upper quadrant was, I am relieved to say, returning to normal. I probed inside my mouth with my finger just to make sure.

The hansom swayed and jolted along a narrow ridge, barely wide enough to take the carriage, the wheels churning up snow, spitting out shards of ice that tumbled down to the chasm beneath. Sir John Franklin decreed the emergency past and chose to dematerialise, my fortuitous meeting thus ended.

'I shall not tarry longer than is necessary, Wilkes, for I know Hélène be set on a fair course for the principality of Volknik. God speed and good luck to you, sir.'

The bulb handle of his walking cane shone for a while like an opal aflame with pleasantly meandering colours and then he was gone, taking his frost and cold air with him, the interior of my cab returning to a more pleasantly warm temperature.

* * *

Hospital Report

'A period of stability. Bandage him up. We as medical men have done all we can. But the patient remains critical. We have successfully operated and removed those deadly splinters from the soft tissue, anyhow.'

'Will he be a vegetable case, professor, alive but in a vegetative state? Are we dealing with simply concussion or deep damage to the frontal lobe? I dread to dwell too much upon this, but he and his bicycle were wrapped round the front wheel of a motor-omnibus.'

'Care and rest, doctor. It is in God's hands now.'

* * *

At dusk I arrived by hansom cab to begin my journey on the forest railway that would eventually take me to the village of Karstein, the horse being remarkable for it had travelled cheerfully for mile after mile without needing to be watered or requiring hay, and appeared to be as fresh at the end of the journey as at the beginning, nudging me with her amiable muzzle as I stroked her silky mane.

There was a pause of time before the train came in and, sitting on the platform bench, smoking my pipe, I was surprised that here in the principality of Volknik at least it was pleasantly autumnal and that the plummeting temperatures and frozen wastes of the plateau appeared to be a long distant memory. Here was I, a little battered, surely, but nonetheless dry and warm and my bowler and gabardine coat passably wearable, although the uppers of my brown brogues could have done with a good polish for my shoes had been waterlogged for so long.

Reaching for my furled umbrella, and getting up, for a distant whistle indicated the train was due, I could not help overhearing a conversation taking place in hushed tones between a porter and his station master.

'Herr Keller, I hear from my cousin in Karstein that wolves have come closer to the village and have been baying at the moon.'

'Ha, the scalliwags. Well, Olaf, the train is in, best load the gentleman's luggage. Mustn't keep Herr Kessner the engine driver waiting.'

'Of course, Herr station master. I shall do as you say.'

'Where are you bound, sir?'

'The Block and Stake Inn. It is recommended in my Bradshaw's *Guide*,' I replied, fumbling in my pockets as I took out my ticket to be clipped.

'Fine establishment and excellent food. Herr Bauer and Netta will look after you, I'm sure.'

After travelling across the frozen northern plateau, for part of the journey at least with the benefit of a fast, efficient GNR steam locomotive, I was surprised to find the forest light railway consisted of trains being hauled by little narrow-gauge engines.

'But the wolves of Karstein,' continued the still perplexed porter, placing a wooden crate of live chickens and some boxes of apples in the special luggage coach, 'there are those who regard wolves as an evil omen.'

'Black dogs then, the lot of 'em. Superstitious tittle-tattle, a lot of spook rot. Now you have a safe journey, sir, and do please give my fondest regards to Herr Bauer at the inn.'

The station master hastily ushered me into a compartment and, slamming the door shut, gave me a last cheery wave before signalling his porter for the train to depart. The carriages were, by GNR standards, somewhat antiquated circa 1862, although each compartment appeared sumptuous for that era with glass crystal lamps, tasselled blinds and comfortable cloth-covered seats. The interior was mahogany panelled and very lavish in period style. The lamps beneath the luggage rack flared and hissed continuously, compressed gas, I surmised, providing the lighting for this forest trip.

The porter shouted out, 'Karstein terminating at Vratnik,' and, as he waved a green lamp, the train steamed off.

'Hello. By your bowler, regimental gabardine coat and furled umbrella, I perceive you are English, sir,' said a blonde young lady, wearing a bonnet and travelling cloak, sitting opposite. 'My name is Katrina Blaufelt, by the way.' She smoothed her voluminous skirts and smiled sweetly. 'Have you come far?'

'I am glad to make your acquaintance. My name is Humphrey Wilkes and I am from Cambridge. I work at a faculty there, although I've been up north for a while.'

'Oh my, this is your first trip to our beautiful forest?'

'Indeed, I have been planning a holiday in the principality of Volknik for some time. Leipzig is not so far, and the village of Karstein is noted for its fine ale and picturesque setting.'

'Vratnik, of course, has a handsome castle, and the mountains are really quite spectacular.'

As the train rattled along, the winter light was fading fast and the view from the carriage window of fir trees whizzing past became more and more of a gas-lit liquid reflection of my somewhat haggard face in the glass. Katrina prattled on as young ladies are wont to do, while I took out my briar-root pipe and smoked awhile.

I recall, when the train was winding its way along the forest interior and about to enter the mouth of a tunnel, a queer thing happened. The gas jet ensconced in the crystal glass dimmed above Miss Blaufelt's head and, as we plunged into a dark tunnel the light flickered and, with a stab of horror, I saw her undulating face transformed from being extraordinarily pretty into something ugly and malevolent. Once out of the tunnel the young lady became herself once more.

Some twenty minutes later, the train rounded the curve at Karstein's pretty little church and entered the station. I was, to be honest, glad to get out of the compartment but remained polite and sociable as if nothing untoward had occurred.

'Goodbye, madam,' I said cordially, raising my bowler hat and giving a slight but stiffly formal bow in the Germanic way.

'Goodbye, Herr Wilkes, be careful, I hear there are lots of hungry wolves on the prowl,' she laughed, kicking the sharp heels of her shapely boots against the compartment seat in a little drum roll. 'Do make a special point of visiting Vratnik Castle,' she called out as I waved. 'I am told it is really quite olden and the peasants thereabouts fear it greatly.'

Herr Bauer from the Block and Stake Inn was waiting to greet me on the platform of the chalet style station. He was smoking a large pipe, and wore stout socks and lederhosen.

'A pity it's already dark,' said he, receiving my portmanteau and carpet bag from an officious porter. 'Our forest looks so wonderful in autumn colours. Welcome to Karstein, Herr Wilkes.'

Making our way up the cobbled street in a wagonette, whose wheels creaked and clattered at every turn, the jovial innkeeper talked fondly of his little village and how lovely was the time of year. The inn, its latticed windows ablaze with lamplight, looked most cheery and welcoming, this despite the gruesomely painted inn sign dangling by its squeaky iron brackets above the door that hinted of a historic place of execution nearby.

At this warm and commodious hostelry introductions were made. Netta, it turned out, was the innkeeper's wife. Fraulein Lottie and Hildegard served behind the bar. A small crowd of friendly regulars were sat drinking steins of beer in front of a large stone-carved fireplace, with a heap of logs crackling in the grate. Whilst a flurry of sparks spat out over the tufty hearth rug, merry laughter was to be heard and the convivial chink of glasses. All passed most pleasantly. I was shown my room upstairs along the landing but later a brief altercation took place that was to leave a fundamental impression upon me.

Herr Bauer, I recall, was showing me his hunting gun with the engraved stock displayed upon hooks above the fireplace, whereupon Netta gleefully returned from the beer garden clutching a small wicker basket. About to enter the kitchen, she hesitated, putting aside some bunches of winter greens.

'See Willi, look what a prize I found growing in our vegetable patch. When hollowed out it will make a most splendid little lamp and our kitchen shall soon be sweetened by its warm, rich smell when I bake a crusty pie.'

'Never!' screamed Herr Bauer, snatching the modestly sized pumpkin from her basket and hurling it out of the inn door in a fit of incandescent rage. It landed with a dullish splat outside. 'I will not, will not, I say, have that – that thing in my inn!'

I confess I was most puzzled by the innkeeper's stormy outburst.

'You know All Hallows is nearly upon us. What on

earth provoked you to such heights of foolishness?' bellowed the irate fellow, beside himself with rage.

'My pet, what harm can there possibly be? It is, after all, only a weeny one.'

'So, what happened to Klaus, Herman, Joanna, Heinz and Frederick last October was merely light comedy, a farce?'

'No, no, Willi, forgive me, I only meant to cook a little...'

What more was there to say? Netta rushed up the staircase in floods of tears, her sobs could be heard even from her bedroom upstairs.

'You silly blockhead!' the innkeeper shouted furiously at the timber-framed ceiling. 'Really, woman, has common sense deserted your reason? Do you not recall the dire warnings from Dr Klaus Kleinz at the Medical Institute no less? Really, woman, whatever next?'

Herr Bauer shook his head despairingly and disappeared into the kitchen. I was both astonished and yet I confess sympathetic to this outburst.

A roast boar was prepared for supper and, whilst I ate my meal in the convivial nook specially set aside for diners, Herr Bauer, his temper once more restored, enjoyed a period of jovial banter, telling me of his hunting of wild boar and black bears in the forest. The principality of Volknik was a mecca for wildlife and he insisted I accompany him on a trek into the mountains as part of my stay. My delicious meal finished, I took out my pipe and tobacco pouch and leant back in my chair, a truly content and well-fed individual, for after my expedition into the frozen north I positively welcomed pleasant, companionable argument and cosy domesticity, for it reminded me of Cambridge.

'Herr Bauer,' I asked, sipping the frothy head of my beer stein. 'Whatever happened earlier with Netta?'

He lit his own pipe – a handsome calabash – and, pausing to consider a wreath of tobacco smoke ascending ceiling-wards, appeared frank and to the point.

'A spat – how you English put it, Mr Wilkes. A man and wife will argue over the silliest things. You're a bachelor, I take it. Well, I lost my temper with Netta over a trite matter concerning an autumnal fruit.'

'I know that much,' I chuckled, warming to mine host immeasurably. 'You damn well chucked it out the door.'

'More beer, Herr Wilkes?'

'No, no, no – stay put. What I have to say may be of some relevance. In our country, at least, the pumpkin is a celebrated harvest fruit, a gourd. Like New England in the Americas, for example, it is often carved out and decorated, or as Netta suggested, used as a pumpkin lantern.'

'Certainly, I understand wholeheartedly.'

'Part of the autumn festivities not to be shunned.'

'Not in our village,' the innkeeper said, scowling. 'In Karstein, such folly would put our very lives in danger. Anyhow,' he sighed, 'let's change the blessed subject. We must get you kitted out for hiking and cycling. That bowler hat and gabardine coat are hardly country wear. Also, I trust your stay in our principality shall be both pleasant and productive regarding your scientific studies. I must, incidentally, introduce you to Dr Klaus Kleinz over at Karstein Medical Institute. Why, you are both of you university men and should get along like hot potatoes.'

'I'd be honoured,' said I, but first I was concerned to get something off my chest. 'May I have your complete confidence, Herr Bauer?'

'Of course, Herr Wilkes.'

'I must tell you plainly that I myself witnessed something

rather queer and inexplicable upon my train journey over here this evening. A young Fraulein, Katrina Blaufelt.'

'Go on.'

'Her face underwent a peculiar transformation before my very eyes.'

'Is that so?'

The innkeeper took out his leather pocket pouch and started to refill his calabash pipe, tamping down strands of tobacco within the long bowl. He relit his pipe, savouring the smoke as it curled up to the oak-beamed ceiling.

'Yes, into a pumpkin – excuse me, rather, her face took on pumpkin-like features, hideous abnormalities, leathery skin of warty texture, jaggedly pointed teeth. It was only a glimpse, mind, but abominable enough.'

'You really saw this?'

'I did. I do not exaggerate, Herr Bauer.'

'You are certain?'

'Absolutely.'

'My dear fellow.' Tears were welling up in the innkeeper's eyes. He clasped my hands in both of his, overwhelmed by emotion. 'You've just no idea what a relief this is to me. You will not now, I trust, think of me, or any of us come to that, as how you English put it, pathologically insane, when I tell you frankly our village is cursed.'

'Cursed? Well, I must say I have journeyed extensively across the great frozen plateau further north and experienced many strange things, as yet unexplained by science, so I am not entirely unused to baffling else eccentric manifestations, Herr Bauer.'

'From long ago, God knows why, but each Hallowe'en they come to our village to claim more victims.'

'They?'

'The 'pumpkinarals', these horrible mutations.'

Not long after this conversation a local, whom Herr Bauer introduced as Peter Gisz, a woodcutter living in a tumbledown cottage on the outskirts of Karstein village, ambled in from outside. He was one of the regulars come in to enjoy a stein of best beer.

His wrinkled, sun-bronzed skin spoke of a lifetime spent outdoors in the forest. He was, I was told, of a great age and normally very surly and unapproachable, apart from when making his nightly visit to the inn, where he liked to talk with other old-timers who frequented the bar.

'I am cooking up such a pie, Willi.' Netta was, I observed, timidly poking her head round the kitchen door, showing everyone her floury fingers. 'It is fleshy and succulent to eat.'

Herr Bauer looked at her coldly for he had still not forgiven his wife her earlier transgression.

'Pie? Tell me more about this pie,' implored Peter Gisz, drooling down his stubbly chin, for he was obviously hungry and wished to sample a portion.

'A turnip pie,' Netta explained, desperate to get back in her husband's good books, for as Lottie was fond of saying, 'a way to a man's heart is through his stomach.'

'Thank the Lord for that,' answered Herr Bauer, somewhat pacified. 'We have a plentiful supply of winter vegetables in store, anyhow.' He paused to relight his calabash.

'A large slice for me.' Old Peter Gisz raised his foaming stein in a toast to Netta's redoubtable cooking skills.

* * *

Hospital report

'The patient takes a turn for the worse. I forewarned you of this, matron. The brain is an uncommonly tricky organ. A

delayed shock has sent his heart into apoplexy. Let us introduce a calming neurological sedative to stave off the worst tremors. I may yet be forced to operate, but I should not want to re-open the capping of the skull at this juncture. Rest and recuperation remain paramount if Wilkes is to survive. However, the next few hours shall prove critical. I may yet instruct the orderlies to prepare an ice bath and get the theatre ready for my next invasive surgery.'

* * *

'Herr Wilkes of Cambridge, may I welcome you most cordially to my principal domain, the Karstein Medical Institute, affiliated to Leipzig University, by the way, which I am proud to say I attended as a dedicated student and graduated there. Why are you here in our principality?'

'On holiday. I had planned to stay in Karstein for a few weeks and got waylaid upon the frozen plateau up north. It took me a devil of an age to reach my original holiday destination, and here I am, Dr Kleinz.'

'The inn is to your liking?'

'Herr Bauer is a warm and hospitable host. I have only praise for both Frau Bauer's cooking and the standard of my board also. I remain, after my delicious dinner and bar conversation, a contented man.'

'A cigarette?'

'Thank you, I will.'

'But Herr Bauer mentioned on the telephone you witnessed a change occur. An attractive young woman, a Miss Blaufelt. Here, allow me to light that for you. You are an inscrutable man of science? Would you take a glass of Schnapps?'

'Dr Kleinz, I shall be perfectly frank. As a Cambridge microchemist, a man of science certainly, the various events

I have experienced on my travels in the frozen north over the past month have altered my somewhat limited view of life. I am neither religious nor do I crave religion, and yet I have seen things with my own eyes that I cannot for the life of me explain logically. In short, I am hardly shockable. You may with perfect equanimity, I hope, confide in me. For the reason I have been summoned here to your most excellent institute I suspect concerns these queer mutations referred to as 'pumpkinarals'.

'Steel yourself, Wilkes, bring along your Schnapps, there's a good fellow. Come yonder into my little morgue, I have something that will interest you. The corpse is dreadfully withered, but I have done my damnedest to embalm and preserve the specimen over time.'

'Here, let me help you with that rubber sheet. It's nice and tidy in here, Dr Kleinz. Is there a nurse at the medical institute?'

'Carl is my orderly and Fraulein Vertz does for me. She is a most assiduous cleaner.'

'Attractive?'

'I'm afraid not. Careful, careful, the specimen is dangerously fragile.'

'Good grief!' I exclaimed. 'You've carried out a dissection. The top of its orangey, thick skinned, warty head is neatly sawn through. You are a talented anatomist, Dr Kleinz. A very fine job.'

'Thank you, Wilkes. What do you make of my corpse?'

'I'd best describe what we have here as a mutant.'

'That's a first-rate description. You English are good at classifying. Go on. Imagine I'm the editor of *The Lancet*.'

'If I were submitting a paper, I'd say we are on dangerous ground. Not to me, you understand, but a practical no-nonsense medical journal would be sceptical of this mutated human specimen. Even with carefully verified supporting colour plates. But I concur the gash of a mouth undoubtedly possesses the prominent fangs of the vampire species.'

'And there's more, Wilkes.'

Dr Kleinz excitedly gathered a bulky and cumbersome solenoid battery and, attaching wires which he had at some stage surgically introduced to the specimen's warty jugular vein, switched on the current and we watched, fascinated, as the orangey-skinned head lit up and the eyes gleamed menacingly. I jumped back, startled, as the prone corpse began to stir upon the marble slab and a grasping hand reached out to touch my thigh.

* * *

The inn door slammed open and all eyes, including my own, turned to see a tall giant of a fellow, wearing an official helmet, sporting clanking, spurred jack-boots and a most impressive high-ranking uniform jacket of green serge with bright gold buttons and wide, tasselled epaulettes, enter the drinking parlour. His serious demeanour spoke to me at least of long hours of commanding men and overlooking their duty roster.

'My usual bottle of Hertzog Lager,' he called out to Lottie, hanging up his spiked tin helmet and coming over to the fire to warm his hands.

'Good evening, Police Chief Grumm,' exclaimed the innkeeper in a frenzy of fussy platitudes, getting up at once to receive his esteemed guest. He filled von Grumm's stein liberally and made certain his friend was comfortably seated by the hearth.

'Well we are fast approaching Hallowe'en, and despite consulting Dr Kleinz, the leading authority on these pumpkin mutants, neither I nor my men are any nearer to fathoming out a way to protect the village from this annual curse – I am at my wits' end,' admitted the police chief, upending his beer stein and drinking deeply.

Peter Gisz stretched his long bony legs and, warming the worn soles of his old work boots on the brass fender, expostulated: 'My dear von Grumm, in my long life I have never myself actually encountered what we country folk call 'pumpkinarals', but my advice, for what it's worth in this modern age, is upon the night of October 31st stay at home, lock all doors and shutters and retire with a keg of the best Karstein beer to read the family Bible until dawn breaks. That offers protection, I'm sure of it. A statue of Holy Mother or a crucifix placed outside the door will likewise see them off.'

'And you practise what you preach, old fella?' asked von Grumm doubtfully.

'Well, let us be realistic. As I say, I have never seen these creatures. If they were born of the forest I would surely be the ideal person to have an idea of their whereabouts, so we could trace and destroy them.'

'True, true,' admitted the police chief gravely.

'Dr Kleinz from the medical institute insists he has dissected one of these 'pumpkinarals' so they must exist,' the old woodcutter emphasised.

'I have myself seen the specimen you refer to,' said I, lighting my pipe, tossing the spent match into the grate. 'And very startling it was too! The brain matter however was mush – just a mass of fibre. No sign of any human tissue, no grey matter to speak of. The whole body's construction is a puzzle. What's more perplexing is that the limbs appeared to respond to stimuli – in this case, an electrical current.'

'Have you, an Englishman, anything to offer regarding this annual curse? Any fresh perspective?'

I puffed thoughtfully on my pipe. 'The curse is an enigma certainly, but has it ever crossed any of your minds that the forest railway running from Gertz might have a part to play in all this speculation . . . ? At least where it terminates?'

'The forest light railway has served our woodland community since 1862. Whatever put such a vacuous idea into your head, Herr Wilkes?' expressed Herr Bauer with a confused look.

'Wait!' Von Grumm demanded attention. 'This English fellow may have a valid enquiry in the offing. You are meaning to tell us, Herr Wilkes, that the terminus at Vratnik could provide a useful clue?'

'The castle, Herr Police Chief. Vratnik Castle. Wherever I am on my travels I have heard mention of this imposing edifice.'

'The berg is set upon a craggy mountainside and overlooks the village and railway station. It is of interest to tourists visiting the principality, I suppose.'

'It is of interest to me,' I emphasised, knocking my pipe out on the stone hearth. 'And it should be to you, also. Who lives there, anyhow, or is it just a ruin?'

'A ruin? Really, the Baron Reitz and his wife live there. They are treated like royalty though seldom seen or heard of. But that is surely the way with a baronetcy, for he owns much of the land and estates round these parts.'

'Are you in his pay? Speak plainly.'

'Certainly not, whatever are you inferring? The local police force is entirely independent.'

'I rest my case, then, Herr Grumm, but I myself would begin an investigation at Vratnik. Take this Katrina Blaufelt, for example. The lady-mutant sharing my carriage – she was, I know, bound for Vratnik. A coincidence?'

'Well,' sighed Herr Grumm, wearied by his long hours of mentally taxing research into the problem and desperate to find a practical solution. 'What you say offers certain interesting possibilities. I suggest there is no time like the present. Willi, are you up for an expedition to Vratnik? No trains are running at this time of night so we shall have to hoof it.'

'Who are *we*?'

'Yourself, the good English gentleman and myself, Chief of Police Grumm.'

'Our journey into the forest interior will require plenty of sustenance… Netta?' Herr Bauer called out to the busy kitchen. 'Prepare flasks of coffee and pack thick slices of pie wrapped in greased paper with plenty of boiled duck eggs into my rucksack. We will be leaving shortly.'

'Bless my soul, where are you stout fellows headed this time of night?' asked the harassed housewife, pulling on her oven gloves, stooping down low to open the range door with its intense blast of heat almost scorching her face.

'Vratnik, we have urgent business to attend to there. Not a word to anyone, mind. You will be left in sole charge until my return in the early hours of the morning.'

'Of course, dearest, whatever you say. The pie is now freshly baked and the crust browned and crispy. Can you smell it, Willi?'

'Yes, yes delicious, I'm sure. Now get on with it, woman.'

'Cut me a large slice, too,' insisted old Peter Gisz, giving the fire a poke, concerned with watching the flames roar up the chimney, a shower of wood sparks scorching the tufty hearth rug.

* * *

The wolves, I knew, were following our every step, yellow baleful eyes staring at us from beyond the fir trees, the wily animals plodding along beside the road, keeping well out of sight but a constant feral presence nonetheless.

There was at this time of year a distinct frosty nip to the air, the crunchy carpet of fallen pine needles, leaves and twigs crackling loudly, snapping underfoot.

A half hour or so into our excursion, von Grumm shone his bicycle lamp into a wooded clearing, where could be seen distantly glowing lights peeping from the slats of shuttered windows.

'Vratnik village,' intoned the police chief as we gathered round. 'The station is down that yonder hillock. See where I'm pointing my lamp.' But my eyes were focused on something far more imposing and magisterial set upon a mountainous crag, perched high above us. The castle, the old keep of Berg Vratnik, ever watchful like some grim sentinel, a forbidding presence up there in the mountains that could be seen for miles around. I inwardly shuddered at its dark and peculiarly menacing aspect.

We continued our journey and clambered down a steep, earthy bank riddled with gnarled, twisty tree roots, to the railway beneath. Using this monstrous root system as convenient footholds allowed us safe passage and we eventually began a trek following the old line of wooden sleepers and gleaming railway until we reached the darkened, silent platforms of an alpine chalet-styled terminus, surrounded on every side by the moonlit mountain range, the peaks at this time of year dusted with the first falls of snow.

'Hark at those wolves,' exclaimed a concerned Herr Bauer, the innkeeper, no worse for his exercise. 'I wonder if Herr Baron is at home? I can see no lights burning from down here.'

'Castle Vratnik remains shrouded in darkness. One never can tell whether the baron and his wife are in residence,' admitted the police chief. 'Ah, let us pass across the tracks to the goods yard. I see an engine shed and I can see our English holiday tourist straining to peer inside. There will be nothing remotely interesting. The locomotives are stored within a smoky, sooty place where they get coaled and fired. A cigar, Herr Wilkes?'

'Thank you, police chief. My, my, the shed door is stiff. The autumn dampness must have expanded the planking.'

There followed a scraping screech as we finally managed to heave the stubborn door across the concreted step. What confronted us in that gloomy, coal-encrusted sanctum of steam was truly astounding. The twin locomotives fell into insignificance beside the glorious vision of grandeur and pomposity from another age that we encountered.

'A golden coach, intricately carved. See the jewel-encrusted doors glittering by the beam from my torch? A golden coach so lavish and handsomely decorated it could belong to a crown prince.'

'Rubies, emeralds – such an antiquated folly. A family heirloom, I shouldn't wonder. I mean to say, a coach such as this is ill-sprung and hardly fit to travel any great distance. Wait, Herr Grumm, Herr Wilkes, come round here at once. Just look what's inside, resplendent behind the glass. A giant pumpkin!'

* * *

The following morning, the 29th October, I came down to breakfast at my usual nook, not in the best of tempers for I had a splitting headache and had undergone a considerable shock of nerves due to an encounter of the very worst kind.

Herr Bauer and the police chief were already seated at a table in the tiny restaurant, being waited on by Netta and Lottie.

'What a pumpkin!' the innkeeper explained to his wife, helping himself to another frankfurter. 'The largest I ever saw, a true giant. What d'yer make of that, Netta?'

'How many pies could I bake with it?'

'No, forget the pies, it's the size that was incredible. Its girth was truly tremendous and there it was, plumb lording it over everything. It quite took my breath away.'

'An awesome sight,' agreed von Grumm, buttering a slice of rye bread with his knife. 'Herr Wilkes will, I am sure, agree that our best bet would be to get a shot at it with a cannon. But that extravagant golden coach is worth a fortune. To intervene I should have to have the coach requisitioned and that's a mountain of form filling, and legal permission should have to be granted from Leipzig Bureau before us, the police, could budge an inch.'

'But if we could somehow pulp that giant pumpkin we might destroy this Hallowe'en curse once and for all.'

'Oh please, please save it!' Netta now seemed in her squeaky voice to be pleading clemency on behalf of the thing. 'All that plump cooking flesh mustn't go to waste. I am quite as excited as Willi. You must, I say, conserve not destroy this behemoth of a pumpkin. Bring it back home to the Block and Stake, whole and in one piece on the back of our wagonette.'

'Don't be so woolly-headed, Netta,' the innkeeper said seriously. 'This mega-sized autumnal fruit may have the supernatural capacity to kill us. We just don't know what we're dealing with yet. We're not talking about an ordinary show squash that wins top prize in some village marquee. For goodness sake, fetch us some more of those flavoursome frankfurters, and keep your silly ideas to yourself. We did not risk life and limb last night just for some trite quest to fill a woman's oven range so she can thus bake on an industrial scale. Pass me some of that excellent scrambled egg, will you, there's a good fellow.'

Later, Peter Gisz arrived at the Block and Stake and, once settled in his usual fireside chair, ordered a stein brim-full of lager. After wiping the froth from his lip, he offered more pronouncements on the festival of Hallowe'en.

'The crucifix is the only way to defeat these things. Mark you, the old way is the best. That one in the market square, or a roadside crucifix with its little pitched roof, something like that propped up against one's front door.'

'The old tried and tested method against the vampire, certainly, but a mutant? No, I think, Peter, your precuations would prove somewhat ineffectual.'

'I would love to stab Mr Pumpkin with my largest kitchen knife and carve out a big slice of sweet flesh,' laughed Netta, winking at Hildegard and making stab-stab-stabbing gestures.

'I must confess,' said I, filling my old briar pipe and removing to a bar-room chair, 'something truly horrible happened to me last night.' All eyes were drawn towards me.

'Feel free, Herr Wilkes. The more horrible the better,' chuckled Herr Bauer, much intrigued by my admission.

'Last night, after we returned from Vratnik and I had retired to bed, I saw Katrina Blaufelt – but not in the normal sense.'

'A tryst, eh? Go on, young man, love will find a way. You held hands.'

'How romantic,' gushed Netta, completely misunderstanding. 'You agreed to meet secretly, here in Karstein, smuggled her up to your bedroom, eh?'

My cheeks, I confess, reddened considerably, and my mouth felt dry and spongy.

'Outside my bedroom.'

Everyone guffawed the louder.

'No, I meant outside the window. The shutters were not drawn properly, else secured. I saw a silhouette, a hazy shape tapping urgently at the glass pane.'

'But, Herr Wilkes, look old fellow, that's three floors up,' pointed out the innkeeper.

'There's no drainpipe to climb, and precious little ledge,' added the police chief, finishing his breakfast. 'And no convenient tree branch either. That really is odd. An ordinary person would be killed if they were to fall from such a height.'

'Well, odd or not, I jumped out of bed and went over to the window. There was her sly laughter and I knew at once it was Katrina waiting out there for me. "Blaufelt here," I heard her call from behind the window.'

' "Go away!" said I, "I'm tired."

' "You're not scared, are you, Herr Wilkes?" Her impudence made my blood boil. "Of a beautiful, sensuous young woman, I mean."

' "No, madam, I am not."

' "Am I not attractive to you, Englander? My new bonnet fails to rouse you from your stuffy and repressed Cambridge temperament."

' "Look here, young lady, you go too far!" I was patently aghast. However, to my shame, I confess I did approach the bedroom window and open the latch, allowing what looked to be, upon first appearance, a most alluring and pretty young woman to bestride the windowsill, but latterly in a whirl of garish orange a horrid, tough-skinned, warty creature tried to force its way in! The swollen face, recomposed from a leathery fibrous matter, possessed a maw full of uneven jagged teeth that with wanton alacrity sought to clamp down upon my exposed wrist. Still, using all my strength, I managed to shove the execrable changeover being or whatever back outside, closing the window and securing the shutters promptly.'

The police chief nodded: 'A narrow escape then?'

'Indeed, Herr Grumm.'

'Well, I think it a fine tale well told.'

'It's not a tale, Herr Bauer, it really happened,' I insisted, annoyed by the innkeeper's dismissal of my very real experience.

'Can you say for certain you did not dream it? I mean to say, it's an awfully long way up for a young lady to climb to reach your bedroom window.'

'Katrina Blaufelt's not a lady in the normal sense.'

'Of course, Herr Wilkes.'

'They called such visitations ghosts in my day,' pointed out Peter Gisz, puzzled by all the fuss.

'Katrina's not a ghost.' I bit my bottom lip. Time to shut up. 'Forgive me, a ghost is as apt a description as any, Herr Gisz,' I relented.

'A dream – dreamt it all,' Herr Bauer insisted. 'Too much of Netta's famous turnip pie and all that excitement of the golden coach, I expect.'

The innkeeper went behind the bar to collect some crates full of empty beer bottles from the cellar, but paused before he went downstairs.

'Netta, do you think our Mr Wilkes is in love with this forest girl Katrina, after all?'

'Oh stop, Willi. The young gentleman's gone into a huff, don't rib him so.'

The police chief Grumm tut-tutted and got up from his fireside chair to stretch his legs.

'Now, now,' added the mischievous innkeeper, returning and fondly patting my shoulder. 'My dear Wilkes, the Block and Stake is your home for the foreseeable future, and Netta and I are delighted to have you. I meant only to point out the possibilities of love interest by means of a jest.'

'That's it!' I jumped from my chair, nearly knocking the spectacles off the end of my nose, all embarrassment forgotten.

'You *are* in love with Katrina, then?' Netta enquired.

'No, not at all. Listen – how stupid we've been. The answer's been staring us in the face all along. It's your dratted inn sign that holds the key to this mystery.'

'What the devil are you on about now, Wilkes?'

'I have it at last, gentlemen. Whereabouts is this historical place of public execution depicted on the Block and Stake's painted sign, Herr Bauer?'

'Why, the market square, that's where they used to burn –'

'Witches.'

'And execute –'

'Heretics.'

'Oh dear, it's just too bloodthirsty to go into now, Herr Wilkes,' said the innkeeper, giving his wife an anxious glance. 'It all happened a long, long time ago. The village of Karstein wanted to forget, pretend nothing had happened, a shameful event in our principality's history. A few old pieces of parchment documenting the trials of witches and so forth are kept at our local history museum, in the office, I believe.'

'Of no importance,' muttered the police chief. 'Old witchcraft papers. We shall, I fear, require sterner stuff than that to defeat our Hallowe'en visitors. Old myths and legends, hearsay. No, our best option is somehow to destroy that giant pumpkin. Is it like a nesting queen bee, I wonder, nurtured and protected because of its importance?'

'I too suspect the giant pumpkin, my dear police chief Grumm, but, pray tell me, where exactly is this museum?'

'Why, just up the road. Professor Weiner from Leipzig University is its honorary curator and he is visiting at present. Shall I telephone?'

'Please, Herr Bauer, I shall make my own way. Tell him to expect me shortly.'

* * *

I proceeded to walk off my breakfast. I took my time and strolled up the village's cobbled street, past the quaint timber-framed shops, peering at their gaily painted fronts, the rows of painted doves and hearts upon the gables, the queer little carvings of gnome-like creatures and fairies.

Fraulein Hindenburg popped out from the tobacconist's to greet me, bearing a gift of a fine cigar.

'Thank you most kindly, madam,' said I.

'Any friend of Netta Bauer has always a welcome in my heart. Are you going far, dear?'

'The museum, Fraulein Hindenburg.'

'Ach, our museum hosts so many notable artefacts – a spindle, the woodcutter's tools, hedge cutters' gloves, an old kiln, a collection of speckled fowl eggs, ladies' hats and costumes from the seventeenth century onwards.'

Hardly anything to set the enquiring antiquary's pulse racing, but then I was not intending to dwell nostalgically upon old junk all day long.

'Farewell, Fraulein Hindenburg.'

'Good day, young man, and enjoy your hour or so spent at our museum finding out about the history of Karstein.'

Yes, but not the sort of history you're thinking of, I considered to myself, pausing at the wool shop to adjust my bowler hat, check I looked presentable. Suddenly I felt a shock run through my system for behind, mirrored in the reflection from the shop window with its little glass blown whorls, a pretty young lady wearing voluminous skirts, a fetching winter bonnet and leather ankle boots buttoned up the side was grinning at me.

'Katrina, what are you doing here?'

I turned round to face her, mildly annoyed I had been taken unawares like this.

'Warning you not to meddle, Herr Wilkes,' she told me in a husky voice. 'Your fine English ways are not ours. Here in the principality of Volknik, and Vratnik in particular, we have olden rules and we abide by them. And now autumn's here and October with us once more, you would do well to mind your own business. So go away, why don't you, back to Cambridge, back to your faculty. Aren't your work colleagues missing you? Especially I mean your bowler hat, that smelly old pipe of yours and city umbrella.'

'How typical, how utterly facetious. Are there no limits to the depths of your depraved sarcasm, Miss Blaufelt? Why the blazes should the inhabitants of Karstein have to put up with this wretched curse every Hallowe'en?'

'We're not going to simply turn to mush, you just don't know what you're dealing with. I've tried to be awfully nice and friendly, but you're just horrible to me.'

'Nice? You, madam, call trying to bite my wrist last night nice? That was abominably uncivil of you.'

'I only wanted to have a chat.'

'And turn me into a mutant, no doubt. Look, I really must be going. Good day.'

'Where are you hurrying off to now?'

'The museum, Katrina.'

The young woman looked aghast.

'That boring old place. Wait! The big fat crawly spiders are nice. Can I come too?'

I was naturally opposed to this.

'Er, no, as a matter of fact. I'm going to study rare fowls' eggs, make a list of them and draw one or two for scientific analysis,' I lied. Was she fooled by my deception? I doubt it.

* * *

Leaving Miss Blaufelt to her shopping for the latest fashions and lingerie, no doubt, I hurried off to the museum, where I was met by a bewigged, scholarly gentleman wearing a frock coat and spats. He greeted me warmly – one university man to another.

'Glad to meet you, sir, name's Weiner, Professor of Anthropology at Leipzig University, you know. You are, I perceive, Humphrey Wilkes of Cambridge faculty, the microscopic scientist. I have read one of your dissertations – a most ingenious paper, if I may be so bold. You are to be congratulated.'

'Why, you are most generous. Herr Bauer telephoned, I trust?'

'He did. You have come concerning some very rare and hard to find trial papers. I took the liberty of making a thorough search of our historical files. Step this way, Mr Wilkes.'

Inside the museum's office the relevant filing cabinet

was easy to locate. Amongst other papers were a variety of documents in a cardboard box labelled 'Witch Burning'.

I reached inside and retrieved a tatty sheet of parchment, yellow and crinkly with age, nibbled by mice. It was headed 'The Curse of Maria Stromberg – being a complete rebuttal of all charges of sorcery laid against her in the year of our lord 1662.'

'Well, I never did!' said Professor Weiner scratching his chin, bringing over a shaded desk lamp so we could read better. The handwriting was in old Germanic, Lutheran script and Professor Weiner did his damnedest to translate:

> *'You should be thoroughly ashamed of yourself, Herr Baron – you, my once trusted friend and your Lawyer like the others have betrayed me. This is a village of wicked, spineless vipers eager to profit by disclosing to certain informants complete untruths and fabricated evidence to damn me to the flames, on account of a stupid wart, so that my wealth and property might be disposed of to your financial gain. Well, if I am to be burnt at the stake in the market square on Hallowe'en Night – October 31st 1662 – a much troublesome curse will follow from this time forward for many generations to come. After cremation I have requested my good friend plain Mrs Dale to scatter my ashes on my vegetable garden, which has provided me with so many happy hours for the cultivation of prize vegetables. This small favour I am sure you will not deny a harmless female.*
>
> *Yours spitefully, Maria*

'Mein Gott!' he exclaimed, realising at once the severe implications of the document. 'The woman was most certainly a witch after all.' The professor pulled at his walrus moustache anxiously. 'Plain Mrs Dale, eh, spreading her ashes on the vegetable garden indeed, where Maria no doubt grew her prize pumpkins.' He sighed deeply. 'But how can we, the village of Karstein, atone for this centuries-old curse?' he implored, shaking his bewigged head wearily.

'By burning down the engine shed,' I insisted bluntly. For there was no room for indecision this late in the day. 'A party of villagers must, en masse, tonight destroy the golden coach that houses the spirit of this grudge-bearing witch Maria Stromberg, for she and her giant pumpkin, this great gourd, this fruit of vast proportions and an even vaster propensity for evil, are one and the same. I am convinced of it. We must forthwith immolate the shed completely.'

* * *

Hospital Report

'A high fever persists, an abnormally high body temperature, a reaction no doubt to the stronger than normally prescribed doses of medication, Professor Canty. His system is considerably weakened but I fear cranial pressure is another issue. For now I would advise against a second operation to check for scarring tissue and other abnormalities.'

'Fever, you say, Doctor? Well, at least our Mr Wilkes is still breathing. To be brutally frank, I am amazed he has lasted this long, given the profound nature of the fractures, for you will recall he was traumatically crushed by the tyre of this motor-omnibus in South Street.'

* * *

Late that night, after meeting at the Block and Stake and drinking our fill, to excess I must add, we – that is a group of us calling ourselves The Avengers of Karstein, bearing flaming torches – walked down the rough turf path and followed the railway along the track to the goods yard at Vratnik. Buckets of pitch and inflammable oil were liberally used to douse the engine shed and, most crucially, the golden coach housed within. Minutes later a blaze was under way.

'Death to the witch – death to the queen of gourds,' we chanted as one, some of us having drunk so much beer we could barely stand. The lightweight wooden structure ignited and became awash with fire. The heat was intolerable. Soon my face and hands were scorched by the intensity of the blaze and then an explosion of flame occurred and leapt out, nearly engulfing us onlookers, but we were so inebriated we didn't care and laughed and laughed until tears streamed down our hot cheeks.

Acting as kindling, the engine shed roof had caught fire swiftly, sending a flurry of smoke and sparks funnelling skywards up towards the old castle keep of Berg Vratnik.

How I cursed my bowler and gabardine coat that clung to me like a reptilian skin, the clammy material causing me to sweat profusely and increase a feeling of being roasted alive.

Beaten back by the flames, many of us gathered to swig brandy and witness the final upsurge of this grand autumn bonfire from a safe distance.

'Gather the charred pods up when the fire has settled,' I shouted, certain that the golden coach had now been reduced to ash and smoke. 'We must not allow regeneration to occur. The seed pods of the giant gourd, when sufficiently cooled down, can be stacked on the back of Herr Bauer's wagonette and disposed of in vats of acid.'

'Why should the pods not be buried at the crossroads or else a plot of holy ground?' suggested the police chief von Grumm, who had been overlooking operations and at the forefront of the destruction of the golden coach with the giant pumpkin inside, glorified behind glass. 'I shall instruct the padre to prepare a space in Karstein churchyard – the curse of Maria Stromberg is no more, her golden throne room within the giant gourd destroyed.'

'Not buried in any kind of ground, holy or otherwise.' I was adamant upon the point. 'A sulphuric acid bath, the pods must be allowed to disintegrate in vats before being cast out to sea. Follow my instructions to the letter, Herr Grumm. I am not a research chemist at Cambridge University for nothing.'

Before the flames took hold, Maria the witch invisibly flew out of her pumpkin, causing a flourish of autumn leaves to hurtle about the tracks.

'Oh, what is to happen to "old faithful"?' she wondered, watching from above. She could never physically intervene for it was not yet Hallowe'en Night and her powers were at a low ebb, but Maria made a concerted effort to escape and swooped up the mountainside, leaving behind the debacle and the screaming shouts for revenge from the men of Karstein, making instead for the castle battlements of Berg Vratnik. She would 'teach that Mr Wilkes, that arrogant Englishman, such a lesson', Maria thought to herself happily.

* * *

'Shame on you all,' said Netta, stirring the coffee pot next morning, while Fraulein Lottie served the guests in the breakfast room a hearty meal. 'Poor Mr Pumpkin should have been brought back to the inn for me to deal with. I should have carved slices out of him royally and sold my pies all over Germany – and my name would be associated with good eating and I, a firm favourite with the bank manager.'

'Oh, do leave off,' winked Herr Bauer. 'It'd weigh a ton and never fit in to your kitchen. And as for that canny seventeenth-century witch I told you of who nurtured it, why she'd probably have set the place on fire and blown up your precious oven and hanged poor Lottie here upside down in a tub full of cheese-curd just for the fun of it.'

'It was the raging fire that was her final undoing, and you see it protected us against her rage and spell making,' said Professor Weiner from Leipzig University, helping himself to more pickled eggs and sour cream, heaping the concoction onto his plate.

'If it had been Hallowe'en Night the mutants would have tried to shield the pumpkin from harm,' said I, placing a dollop of jam on my black bread.

'Quite so, Wilkes, you're right – all hell would have broken loose if we'd brought the giant pumpkin back here. Believe me, Netta, you're better off without that enormous pumpkin. We all are. Save your precious carving knife for chopping up swedes, beets and turnips for today's lunch.'

'And did you see Katrina?' Lottie wanted to know, pouring out more coffee. 'Did you say hello to your friend, the forest girl, Herr Wilkes?'

She nudged Netta and whispered something – either these women were incredibly naïve or having a laugh at my expense. I saw where this was ultimately leading and tried to put a firm stop to their speculation without success.

'Katrina is far from being an ordinary young lady. She is blonde and very pretty, certainly, Lottie, but she is and will always remain a *mutant*, some kind of shape-shifter with an inbred vampiristic tendency. She is, in plain words, of *mixed race* certainly. I am under the impression she uses her pixie-like charm to great advantage.'

'And you are attracted to each other – admit this is so, Mr Wilkes.'

'Really, Lottie, you and the bar staff are truly exasperating sometimes. Another cup of your excellent coffee, if you don't mind. At least that awful curse is lifted, anyhow. This Hallowe'en should pass as a celebration of harvest home.'

* * *

I decided to spend part of the afternoon trekking through the forest and visiting the mountains around Vratnik. I was intending visiting Leipzig later in the week, and Professor Weiner had cordially invited me to stay the night with his wife and three children at that most delightful of European cities, famous for its fine architecture and musical associations.

The forest was tangy with the scent of pine needles. I was approaching the clearing where the steep, tree-rooted bank led down to the railway line when I heard a rustle of leaves and snapping of twigs as someone approached.

'Who goes there?' I called out, anxious for wolves, for a pack of them lurked close by, I was sure.

'It is only I, Herr Wilkes.' From out of the trees came Fraulein Blaufelt, daintily tripping along a woodland path in her pretty bonnet and voluminous skirts and ankle-length boots. 'I was myself out walking and saw your familiar bowler hat bobbing in the distance. Have a care, sir, for the autumn mists encroach upon the woodland early and make an unsuspecting walker follow the wrong route.'

'The signpost to Vratnik is marked clearly enough,' I said, somewhat irritably. 'Really, Katrina, must you always talk in this mysterious way? You would think I was incapable of looking after myself.'

'If we were to, say, become engaged, Herr Wilkes, then allowing for decorum, having done the proper thing, you could safely take me back to Cambridge with you. I would be pleasurable company sharing your hearth. I could look after you...'

I seized the young lady by the arm.

'Don't hurt me so, Herr Wilkes, let go this instant, I say.'

'You excite me in a way that is dangerous for both of us.' I quickly relented, understanding how serious and possessive I must sound. 'You are a mischievous little pixie, madam. Begone, thou fairest sprite of the woodland dell.'

'Your fairytale, babyish talk eludes me, sir, although you would not, I trust, object to a light peck on my cheek, surely? A fond kiss to celebrate our ongoing acquaintanceship? I am a real woman, after all. Do not, I say, be so stuffy and reserved. It does not become you, Herr Wilkes.'

'I – I – really, Katrina. This is patently outrageous. I mean to say...'

However, I confess the lure of her pretty blonde looks, the way in which the woman coquettishly assessed me with her eyes and drew herself closer, banished all recent memory of her dreadful mutation and consequent aggressive behaviour at my bedroom window, when Katrina had been, God help me, mistakenly 'invited in' for the vile enough purpose of biting my wrist and turning me into one of her kind.

I pressed her petite form close to me. Dear God, I had lost my reason, surely I was a man befuddled, torn by extremes. I kissed her lightly upon the cheek and was transported...

* * *

Hospital Report

'Submersion in the specially prepared ice bath, frozen into a state of suspension. Now his core body temperature is reduced, Dr Worth, Nurse Kitson.'

'Yes, Professor Canty.'

'You will observe, the top of the skull is once more removed, allowing us surgeons access to the soft tissue, the frontal lobe in particular.'

'Went without a hitch.'

'Heart rate much slower than normal,' the anaesthetist remarked.

'Indeed, pass me forceps and a probe. Ah, Mr Adleton, England's foremost specialist in this branch of surgery, you've spotted something, I see. Nurse, more operating light.'

'Well, Canty, I've located our problem, it's natural for the body to reset and here, where my scalpel is pointing, we have a miniscule splinter fragment that has since your first operation worked its way out of the grey matter. It's only visible under magnification. Now, if we can safely remove this little rogue I believe we can rest assured our patient shall be over the worst. His constitution is remarkable, remarkable. That's what was causing pressure on the brain all along!'

* * *

My eyes snapped open with a start. I was lying in a steel coffin. The damp, chill atmosphere made me realise the lid had mercifully been left off for it was propped against the far wall. Speaking of walls, these were built of stone slabs mildewed green and covered by spores of fungi. I felt instinctively I was below ground and knew beyond all reasonable doubt that I was presently encased within the four solid walls of a dungeon. I perceived the tiny hearth built into the wall was unlit, the grate extinct of coals, and I started to shiver uncontrollably.

'Welcome to Vratnik Castle, Herr Wilkes. I trust your stay with us will be short and not too uncomfortable. Ah, incidentally, this is my wife, Irena.'

Most profoundly was I struck by this odd couple. For, in the dingy light afforded by the barred window, I might assume ordinarily they were mother and child, he with his blonde, tidy hair, wearing a maroon frock coat, diamond-pinned kerchief and velvet pantaloons, so tiny and small-boned, propped upon a type of high stool propelled by tiny castors. She tall, well over six feet in height, and slender, so pale did she seem, her skin might have been of the finest porcelain.

'I am most honoured to make your acquaintance, madam,' said I, 'and you, sir, are of course Baron von Reitz, the ruler of the principality of Volknik. Your most excellent castle perched up here on the crag is on the tourist map, but as we approach winter your berg is presumably untroubled by hikers and sightseers, although of course this is a fairly isolated range of mountains. You get a mention in Bradshaws, at least.'

'You, sir, were of course holidaying in Karstein.'

'Briefly, yes. It appears from my surroundings I am now staying at an altogether more prestigious boarding house. Might I trouble you for my pipe and matches?'

'Smoking is strictly disallowed, I'm afraid, Herr Wilkes. My delicate constitution abhors and indeed reacts violently to any form of dust, else tobacco ash. In point of fact, I abhor any kind of ash, and a cloud caused by smoke rising from a burning engine shed far below in the village was particularly galling. Thus, that is why I have detained you here at my castle.'

'Ah, the golden coach. I thought as much–'

'*My* golden coach – the carriage belonged to me, it was my property. I supplied the coinage for its original construction. I oversaw every part of the design and conception.'

'Really, Baron, for a rational person it is not too hard to conclude that your long and noble line of ancestors were at some stage beholden to this witch Maria Stromberg, who for the unlawful acquisition of her lands and wealth, was sent to the stake at the market square on a trumped-up charge of sorcery. Unfortunately as it turned out, Maria actually was a witch and a spectacularly talented spellbinder. She remains amongst us, presumably, as an astral being, very deft at dishing out curses as the von Reitz family must have learnt to their cost.'

'An astral being,' laughed the baron's wife, giving me a look of utter contempt. 'Whatever that may be, Mr Wilkes. No, she is a shape-shifter, a shape-changer, an escaper into various guises. Maria may choose to remain invisible or become full bodied as she wills it.'

'Drat your clever talk, Baroness, I am no expert, a shape-shifter then, if you say so.'

'Beholden to a point, certainly,' said the baron, returning to my earlier remark. 'But all of us are outcasts in our own way, are we not, dearest?'

The baron's wife, so tall and stately, her waxy white physiognomy queerly beautiful, allowed her abnormally rosy red lips to part, revealing extremely sharp canines that creased her bottom lip when she smiled.

'Good gracious, you are a vampire!' I enjoined.

'Both of us are vampires,' Baron von Reitz corrected. 'We have lived here at Berg Vratnik mostly unmolested, quietly getting on with our lives, for centuries. It was I,

Mr Wilkes, who so long ago originally prosecuted an action against Maria, one of the only grave errors I have ever committed in my centuries-long life – or living death, whichever way you mortals choose to perceive it.'

'Us mortals – really, Herr Baron, at least I am clear upon your own allegiances. Here am I inadequately lodged in a mildewed dungeon, occupying one of your not so commodious metal coffins, a little before time I might venture to say.'

'Only a little and I find that particular model looks so much more streamlined with the lid securely pressed down and vacuum sealed, wouldn't you agree, Herr Wilkes?'

'Am I to be buried alive then?'

'Not exactly. Your punishment for burning down my property, for wholesale destruction of my golden coach, is to be sent into exile, to quit my principality forthwith. Exiled – do you hear me, sir? Away to the furthest north, the land of endless snow and the great ice plateau. Fair weather or foul, it's the Pole you're headed for, Herr Wilkes. Oh, and my dear wife insisted your underclothes be washed and ironed, your gabardine coat cleaned, bowler hat likewise brushed and those sensible brogues have been polished immaculately. The bamboo handle of your city umbrella was a trifle loose so I had it firmed up for you. Everything, you will observe, has been placed inside your coffin, though what purpose they will serve where you are going, I am unsure. As soon as the lid is secured, bon voyage, so to speak. You see, my English friend, our species are really quite benevolent and much maligned.'

* * *

Hospital Report

'Shout close to his ear, my dear, he may yet respond. Your work colleague, Mr Wilkes, is in a deep state of coma, an ice pack applied to the back of his head. Remember, none of us doctors can be certain of the outcome, but he at least remains stable and, since the second operation performed by Professors Canty and Adleton, the pressure upon the brain will have been considerably relieved. I have observed a fluttering of the eyelids but the pupils remain severely dilated. In God's hands, we trust... Miss Eldridge, persist – try again, Lucy.'

* * *

The deep, deep cold penetrated my very being. Now I was verily confined, not merely in a wretched stone dungeon, but a blue arched cavern some way down a plunging crevasse. To add infamy to my predicament, ghastly though it was, apart from the ventilation holes to allow a circulation of air, so at least I would not suffocate, the wretched metal lid that Baron Reitz had secured over me by means of a vacuum seal possessed a glass viewing window, thus I was doubly aware of my isolated, freezing environment, but the cold that chilled my bones was so intense and persistent! I presented already a living death – numb to the point that I must look not dissimilar to a living, frozen corpse like Scott or Crozier.

'How long have I been down here?' I wondered, with so little room to shift my body weight. Cursed bed sores and haemorrhoids should be my only painful companions. Baron von Reitz was a cad all right – of the lowest order, and the most cruel and unfeeling individual I had ever met. He was a contemptuous being and I hated him for his subtle hint as to my eventual fate – incarcerated under the sheet ice of the great plateau, coffined inside an icicle-infested cavern. My senses were very much alive to every nuance of my terrible predicament.

'Mr Wilkes, Mr Wilkes, it is I, Lucy. Can you hear me?'

'What?' I murmured. In a state of idleness a stupor had overcome me – what – who, is that?

'Mr Wilkes, can you hear me?' a lady's sweet voice intoned. My heart began to race at the sound.

'Lucy!' I cried. 'Lucy, I am down here in an ice cave. I am coffined and unable to move – or reach out to you.'

'We are coming down – be patient. The water, cold and compacted as ice, would be deadly to our kind should it melt and begin running. We are proceeding cautiously.'

'It is the group of lady vampires and dearest Lucy,' I said to myself. Lucy, who had saved my life on the ice shelf by giving so freely of her own special restorative blood tonic. I peered anxiously through the glass viewing window, up and up my gaze travelled, beyond the cave. The sheer, jagged face of the cavernous, blue-sheeted wall of the deep crevasse funnelled upwards, Lucy's voice allowed to echo and become louder due to the bouncy resonance of the place. But I could see, indeed I could, a group of black-clad commandos – leaping in impossible bounds, clinging to ledge and jagged, icy outcrop, piercing with extraordinary long, red-varnished nails, the sheer drop of many miles.

'Mr Wilkes, can you hear me? It is I, Lucy!'

A booming voice first bounced down from one wall to another of the crevasse before echoing around the cave until my eardrums hurt.

'Yes, yes,' I cried impatiently, 'I heard you the last time, dammit, Lucy. I told you before, I am helplessly coffined.'

'Hold on, Mr Wilkes, I shall be with you presently. Between us, my sisters and I have prepared you an audacious escape.'

Not long afterwards I was witness to an elongated, red-varnished fingernail of impossible length curling itself round and jabbing like an ice pick into the glacial wall. Lucy swiftly followed, clad in a fetching black frock coat and boots, edging herself along a ridge before stooping low and entering the icy cavern where my steel coffin lay alone and abandoned.

Framed in my viewing window appeared a beautiful, long-haired brunette, her kindly eyes brown, almost black in intensity, full of curiosity at my unfortunate predicament. Her angular, pale features creased into a warm smile. A unit of other women vampires arrived and gathered round.

My heart nearly burst. 'Lucy!' I gasped, so pleased to see her. 'Can you fathom this confounded coffin? I suppose we must somehow upraise the lid, but it was securely fastened not by screws but a thick strip of India rubber, forming a vacuum.'

'Really, dearest Mr Wilkes, your naivety is really quite endearing. If I or any of my sisters were to even brush lightly against the outside of the coffin, or by the gentlest of touches hope to raise the metal lid, a clockwork device on the inside would automatically trip a mechanism and a tray of sharpened steel spikes would rise up from the base and impale your back and lower abdomen. You should be stuck like a squealing pig to the base of the coffin – and we can't have that happen, can we?'

'My God, Lucy, the baron has thought of every eventuality. I'm done for!'

'Pshaw! I have encountered a similar funerary artefact. I think it was in Paris. The design was originally conceived by a clever vampire clockmaker, a Monsieur Leven of Grenoble. You must work from the inside, it is perfectly safe that way, Mr Wilkes. You must somehow wedge – jam the switch. Can you feel a small lump under your posterior – oblong like a domino?'

'I can.'

'Like a domino?'

'Understood.'

'You still possess your furled umbrella?'

'Indeed.'

'Lean heavily against the upraised switch and when the compressor activates slide your umbrella – the curved bamboo handle – in the tiny gap, then I can cleave open the lid fairly easily. We can break the vacuum seal at no added risk to yourself. This type of receptacle is, I suspect, one of Monsieur Leven's earlier prototypes.'

'And I'm much relieved to hear it, Lucy. I shall do all you say.'

The commandos were all waiting and ready for action, so it was imperative the switch was activated. I manoeuvred my backside and shifted to the right a little, then of all the luck managed to depress the switch device. I heard a clockwork whirring followed by a loud, resounding 'clack'. I edged the bamboo handle of my brolly into place, wedging it into the tiny gap, causing the mechanism to clamp tightly. To try to reclose it was now impossible. The clockwork whirring re-intensified then wound altogether down.

'Lucy, Lucy!' I could barely contain my joy, as the coffin lid, with a sucking noise, was removed.

I barely noticed my predicament but was rather focused on my pretty rescuer.

'Oh, to see you once again, Lucy, after all this time, warms my heart immeasurably, and your friends, of course.

I owe you all so much.' I attempted to grasp Lucy's delicate hand in mine, an act of affection, of friendship.

'You are a human, Mr Wilkes, have a care, sir. It pains me to say this, but we are of vastly differing physicality.'

'You mean to imply that I should not love you for you are a vampire species? My dearest lady, I owe you my life. Lucy, enough of this, accept my hand and allow me to kiss your own. Why should I be prevented from a simple gesture of knotting our friendship.'

The beautiful creature smiled, and such a smile that radiated a reciprocation of my feelings. Her eyes appeared to glow all the myriad colours of the rainbow. But of course, she was right – an immeasurable gulf lay between us, a gulf I must respect, and after brushing my lips against her outstretched hand I naturally withdrew my love-making, talking of my time in Karstein, explaining in an easy, humorous way all that had occurred.

After being confined for so long, it was terribly hard to extricate myself from that metal coffin. The girls did their best to haul me out, but I had a severe case of cramps and had lost sensation in my toes.

'And did you enjoy your vacation in Karstein?' asked Lucy mischievously, abruptly pulling me upright by my armpits. 'Did the village come up to Herr Bradshaw's standards? It's pumpkin-growing country, so they say.'

'I stayed mostly at the Block and Stake Inn, Lucy, and as a tourist you might say visited Vratnik Castle, but ended up in the dungeon of all places.'

'Kept prisoner at that old berg on the mountainside. Baron von Reitz and his wife Irena live a quiet life at the castle and I've rarely heard mention of them becoming annoyed with outsiders. What on earth have you done to make them angry? Confess all.'

'Well, we're back to pumpkins again,' I confided, 'a giant one – and a golden ancestral coach.'

'Was there a woman involved?'

'Alas for me there was, Lucy, a very clever and unconventional witch, nothing remotely to do with pointy hats and flying broomsticks. Stromberg was her name.'

'So you were spellbound and that's how you ended up imprisoned here below the ice shelf. One of her spells; if so, it is without precedent for a southerner, a witch of all people, to have jurisdiction here in the cold north.'

'No, Lucy, it was the baron and his wife. They exiled me here as a punishment for setting fire to that coach, and destroying their property.'

'Well, that couple, I'm afraid, are very ancient and powerful vampires, they go back a long way, but on the whole mind their own business and keep to themselves. Come autumn much of their income is derived from pumpkins. Did you perchance encounter on your travels any of my kind, apart from the Reitzes, I mean?'

'Strangely, Lucy, pumpkins once again come into play. The medical institute at Karstein has a mortuary which contains a fine example of a kind of hybrid, mummified vampire – a cadaver belonging to a young teenager, partly 'turned' a year or so back.'

'So what was unusual?'

'The head more resembled a gourd, a jack o'lantern, if you will. I enjoyed friendly terms with the local doctor, who had over the years made a study of these queer creatures, and he showed me this preserved specimen. I do not exaggerate, the dermis was tanned orange, thickly skinned and warty. The doctor even possessed a solenoid battery and lit the creature up for me and made it wiggle its arms and legs.'

'How ugly,' Lucy interrupted. 'This poor girl, a teenager

too! Skin like an orange crocodile – yuck! But to return to the present, Herr Wilkes, you are in terrible trouble. North or south, no one dares cross an ancient vampire like Baron von Reitz and get away with it. A witch is nothing in comparison. Is there any place you could escape to – beyond the plateau, I mean?'

'Cambridge,' said I, desperately thinking. 'I have a house and garden there – a job, if I could get back to England. I couldn't bear to think of you being harmed by that evil baron, Lucy – on my account.'

'There is an ice station up by the mountains,' remembered Sharna. 'There is a direct service to England from there.'

'The Great Northern Railway is my only realistic hope of returning to my old way of life. If I can only connect with the express, a Hadley Grange, all will be well with the world.'

'A train stops there once every six months. The service is very spartan out here,' Griselda pointed out.

'Every six months.' I practically gave up on the spot, my heart sank like a stone but fate was, I am pleased to relate, generous for once.

'You are in luck, Herr Wilkes,' Lucy exclaimed happily, doing her best, and succeeding, in cheering me up. 'Directly across the ice field is a range of mountains. The railway you talk of pokes out of a tunnel and winds around its base. The ice station is achievable only with our help, for you are still weak and have no idea of the geography of this place. The timetable board, I am certain, indicates an express due today. A Hadley Grange arrives from the north to take on coal and water and supplies for the kitchen car, and leaves for England tonight.'

'Well, that's a relief. This station is where we're bound then.'

The penetrating cold inside that cavern was painful, nay almost unbearable. The commando girls began frantically rubbing my legs and arms to help restore circulation, and more furs were hastily heaped on my shoulders to conserve precious warmth.

'Lucy!' I blurted out as she bent down and tied up my shoelaces, overcome by strong and ungovernable emotions. 'It is true, we are *blood-linked* are we not, and this enabled you to locate me in this isolated place?'

'Do pipe down, Herr Wilkes, I am concentrating.' Lucy grinned at me and, acting upon some marvellous inner compulsion, gave that steel coffin an energetic kick with her suede ankle boot. It hurtled like a missile over the jutting overhang of the cave's mouth, plunging ever deeper into the turquoise-blue glimmer of the icy abyss far, far below.

She related some interesting biological advances long established in her own species.

'My ears are sonically attuned, I can hear the tiniest sound or reverberation above the plateau, the low rumbling of glacier melt, or breaking pack ice many miles distant.'

'I know I'm a bit backward, you needn't rub it in,' I laughed, 'but what is it you hear now, Lucy, that makes you look so concerned?' I asked, buttoning up my winter overcoat with shivering fingers.

'Why Humphrey, the swish of runners, a surge of activity up there on the plateau.'

''Tis wind sledges,' confirmed Griselda, both the most muscular and broad of the girls, craning her neck to listen. 'Coming our way and hurriedly, too, from the north east.'

'Wind sledges?' I queried, wrapping a thick woollen scarf around my neck and adjusting my spectacles while Sharna helped me on with my gloves. 'Doing what exactly? Are they bounty hunters out for our blood?'

My favourite vampire choked back her giggles.

'Hardly, it is far too early for Baron von Reitz to have alerted Crozier. This hunting party are concerned with prospecting.'

'For gold, oil, minerals?'

'For the graves of past expedition members frozen under the ice. By a process of vampiric transfusion, transfusing the blood directly into the belly button of the frozen corpse by means of a long proboscis that springs from their own navels, unique to this species of Arctic vampire, the hunting party may revive these wonderfully preserved cadavers. The intelligence of the newly exhumed creatures shall vary considerably, but some may prove useful for enslavement purposes where heavy labour is required. I know for a fact that Captain Crozier is overseeing the building of a vast mausoleum at the Pole to house himself and certain high-ranking elders. But why am I wasting time explaining everything to you? Here, see for yourself; allow me to touch the top of your head, Humphrey. Don't be such a baby, it won't hurt. Now close your eyes.'

Lucy gently held a finger to the apex of my skull. I felt a moderate tingling sensation, then came a vision, a mental picture both colourful and alive.

'The wind sledges.'

'Yes, I see them on the horizon clearly, skimming across the ice above us on the plateau. Remarkable.'

'The brand new mausoleum at the Pole.'

There in my mind's eye I glimpsed a vast domed building not unlike the Royal Albert Hall. There were, I noticed, ladders and, wrapped around scaffolding, a number of busy workers attending to its completion.

'Now the unfurling proboscis centred in the belly button I remarked upon, the transfusing of a vampire's blood to revive frozen cadavers. I think this should be of particular interest to a scientist such as yourself.'

'Stop! On an empty stomach that's just too revolting for words, Lucy. No more images of pumping blood into frost-preserved corpses, if you please.'

The living, photographic pictures ceased and I once more opened my eyes to an altogether much nicer contemplation. How lovely was the pretty brunette stood before me, so much so I was moved to say, somewhat mischievously, 'I wonder, Lucy, have you any living colour pictures of yourself I might view, preferably in corsets else nude studies?'

My vampire friend commented thus soberly: 'After long confinement in the steel coffin, Mr Wilkes, I think it prudent not to over-stimulate your imagination.' She flicked my ear playfully with the back of her hand. 'Further, I deduce that your own brain development be not nearly so advanced as ours and not quite so suited to receive these telepathically transmitted images.'

'Bosh! I can receive them perfectly,' said I with feeling.

'Anyhow, let us remove to the surface of the Great Plateau – those advancing sail sledges bode ill.'

Climbing up the deep chimney of the glacial crevasse, assisted by Lucy and her super-agile companions, surely, as we emerged once more onto the flat, broad plain, I saw a half dozen or so of these sail sledges coursing across the snow line. Ideal craft for covering long distances, provided the wind prevailed in the right direction and the way was clear of sastrugi and pack ice rubble.

Every aspect of my daring rescue had been meticulously considered. For cooking purposes, for it was understood that as a non-vampire, in order that I should stay alive, I must obtain nourishment from eating normally, Griselda, by simply concentrating her extraordinary 'ray' vision on a pot full of snow, not only heated water in seconds but magicked up rich, sustaining cuts of seal meat floating in a stew of pemmican. This fatty mash provided me with much needed inner warmth and calories, which brought up my energy levels considerably.

I had hungrily devoured my meal. Lucy was about to assiduously pass me a flask of piping hot tea to slake my thirst, when seemingly out of nowhere one of these nifty sail sleds, possibly a straggler from the rear of the main group, came gliding across the ice to where we were temporarily camped, the wide cut of its runners spraying snow as it slewed round and came to rest. There were three figures on it and all appeared mean and hungry.

A shabbily dressed nautical type wearing a patched up leather jerkin, breeches and old torn, hooped stockings was first to appraise us.

'Gadzooks, what 'ave we 'ere?' The fellow's revolting, crafty face betrayed a need, a despicable yearning, for 'live' blood. 'Plateau's a lonely, miserable place at times, ain't it, gals? To sup, to share a warm wine'd be a real pleasure. I be Silus Tench, one o' the sailors what crewed *Erebus*.'

'Pretty wenches – three, likes of you be thin on the ground,' remarked another, licking his chaffed, blackened lips. 'Name's Snodely. T'was a member o' that ill-fated expedition led by that traitor, Sir John Franklin. My allegiance be to Cap'n Crozier, who bravely marched one 'undred and five stranded souls northward, where Vitus Bering and Chirakov welcomed us into their colony.'

A uniformed officer in a black tricorn hat leapt off the wind sledge and took account of us; imposing his authority, he emitted a fearful howl and drew back his upper lip, revealing yellowish barbed fangs. He pointed a bony, frost-bitten finger in my direction.

'Excuse me, ma'am, who be that lovesick swain cowering behind thy skirts, for I can tell he be born of a most fruitful tree of ripened arteries and veins my men wish to sup deeply thereof? Leave us to take our fill, begone I say, thou womenfolk be fit only for skivvying and bearin' children.'

'You impertinent dogs are evidently unacquainted with civil behaviour. If you, sir, and your cronies' blood were not so tainted with lead, the poison of which radiates from every pore of your putrid countenance, liken to a sooty lamp glass, I should quite fancy a fill-up myself from your own scrawny vine.'

'Cheeky wench, begone, allow us to feed upon this living human.'

Unbelievably, in a breathtaking manoeuvre, Lucy's perfectly manicured fingernail extended almost to the length of a duelling sword, and with unswerving accuracy she plunged the razor-sharp digit through the chest of the officer-class straggler of '48.

Spurting from his torn and filthy tunic, a toxic blood spotted the ice with smouldering droplets. Losing his black tricorn hat, the vampire threw up his arms and fell back, writhing in the snow, kicking out with his feet.

'Barbarous wench!' He gave out a kind of animal snarl. 'You have burst my heart, do not make me headless, I pray thee. My past be agin me an' I'll be bound for Hades.'

'Well, in Hades at least it shall be a good deal warmer!' Lucy exclaimed, withdrawing her sword-stick fingernail and beheading the sailor with one peerless stroke.

While this repulsive wretch began to dissolve, crumble into a soupy mess of crystallised particles, the ragged uniform and buckled shoes all remaining in a heap, the commandos Griselda and Sharna, with sudden savagery, did equal justice to the others, spearing their hearts and cutting off their heads in quick succession.

'Hurry!' called out the female warrior, Sharna. 'We must commandeer the sail sled and thus transport you more conveniently to this ice station, Mr Wilkes. The Great Northern Railway runs a few miles distant below those mountain ranges over yonder.'

We jumped aboard and were soon away. With the sail full and billowing we flew across the ice.

'And what of Captain Francis Crozier?' I shouted above the wind. 'I should not fancy another severe necking from him, I can assure you, ladies.' The ragged scar in the region of my jugular throbbed painfully at the mere recollection of his sudden and violent attack.

Lucy shrugged. 'There be much worse than him.' She spoke up judiciously, keeping her hand firmly on the tiller, her eye on the mountain peaks ahead. 'Those three pups from the hunting party back there were luckily immature and not yet properly developed or capable of inflicting harm upon wiser, more experienced warriors, but those such as Vitus Bering and Chirakov, who migrated here in the early eighteenth century are accomplished and powerful elders definitely to be avoided.'

'How many of the *Terror* and *Erebus* men have you so far encountered, Lucy?' I asked, enjoying the sensation of being whisked along, listening to the runners bite into the icy crust.

'We have fed upon and subsequently destroyed over sixty of the original one hundred and thirty nine, but the high yield of lead in their bloodstream does not agree with our own sensitive palates.'

'Although, to be honest, ma'am, I have upon occasion

enjoyed supping on those expedition members free of lead,' remarked Sharna, the dusky Asian vampire, brushing her tongue across her lips in a most lusty fashion, her almond eyes for a moment becoming luminous and radiating a crimson hue, which required little interpretation.

'1606 was a good year though,' Griselda grinned and stared at my neck dreamily, which I found mildly disconcerting. 'Captain Knight's men of a far superior vintage, eh Sharn?'

Sharna blushed profusely.

Our sledge pushed on, assisted by a favourable wind, skimming ever closer to the range of mountains, the ropes of the billowing sail being competently operated by the frisky Asian vampire.

Suddenly, the mood changed and from quiet introspection everyone was on their guard, looking alert and ready for action – no question. The girls sensed danger with a capital 'D'. Screwing up their noses, the nostrils of which I knew to be ultra-sensitive for prey seeking, they sniffed the air anxiously.

'Be warned, the hunting party has changed direction and is closing in on us – fast!'

'We must cause a distraction, divert their attention.'

'Mr Wilkes, we are going to drop you off. You'd best walk the rest of the way to the station. The Great Northern Railway is just beyond that ridge, and you shall at least be able to follow the snowy imprint of the tracks. From here on in, you must employ maximum effort, Mr Wilkes, bring to bear all of your reserves. I am pretty certain the hunting party, anxious to retrieve their precious sail sledge and avenge the slaying of their comrades, will follow us – not you.'

'Well, I suppose I had better get off and walk, then. I

am not about to argue, Lucy, what you say makes sound sense although I shall miss you ladies terribly. But it is at the ice station I can connect with that dear old locomotive Hadley Grange and attain my passage to England. I am convinced my old life lies in that direction.'

I reluctantly climbed out of the sledge, while Sharna passed me my bamboo-handled city umbrella and somewhat sat-upon, crumpled bowler. I watched, lost in awe, as the craft unexpectedly took off, the sail caught like a kite by the wind, and shot across the icescape. Lucy and I continued to wave until it was just too far to communicate. The other girls kept their heads turned forwards. As a diversion, I trusted their plan would work.

Some time after, I recall the strain of endlessly plodding through the snow affecting my morale, leaving me at an all-time low. The icy wind was cutting through me. I kept wondering over and over if the mountain range was unattainable, the snowy peaks a lost cause. I was, it appeared, on a treadmill, going round and round and getting nowhere and additionally losing more and more body heat. My muscles ached, my throat was parched and restricted, and my face felt moulded from a solid block of granite. My spectacles were as good as useless, the lenses being masked in crinkly ice. The fearful cold refused to relent and my overcoat might as well have been cast from concrete. My poor feet ached terribly, my stout town shoes just about holding up.

It was during this period, this purgatory of frozen numbness, likened to being weighed down by a ton of iron on your back, that something unusual occurred. I sensed now and then that I was being followed, not by a malign presence, you understand, but a guardian, one who actually cared not only for the betterment of my wellbeing but also the successful outcome to the long and perilous journey I had embarked upon some time earlier in my garden back at Cambridge.

Every so often I would crane my neck and see behind me a magnificent polar bear, massive and blubbery, pausing sometimes to shake out its fur, but always keeping a safe distance between us lest I should become alarmed and take fright. The last time I observed the animal's white hide and rolling gait I watched, mesmerised, as all of a sudden this mighty beast sprang up on its powerful haunches, raising its moist black snout in the air, yawning wide its massive jaws as if to roar … but instead projecting a female voice, fragile and full of emotion.

'Dear Mr Wilkes, can you hear me? Humphrey, take heart for we shall meet again soon. Goodbye for now, old thing, and take care. This be Lucy speaking.'

A talking polar bear, not as incredible as it seems, for Lucy and I were *blood-linked*, the stunningly attractive brunette vampire somehow able to shape-shift, to change form out here on the plateau, where every rule of logic and reasonable argument it seems was broken and turned on its head. Polar bear Lucy represented a good omen and intuitively I now felt certain her brilliant diversionary plan had been successful. Thus momentarily buoyed up, I refocused on my quest to reach the ice station, to catch my train home. But, dammit, I admit to being tortuously torn between wanting to be with Lucy and pining for my old life back at Cambridge.

Pausing one last time to watch my dearest enchantress lope back across the tundra, I was tempted to become weepy or maudlin, which anyhow was next to useless and won you no favours out here in this harsh, unforgiving environment. Instead, I gritted my teeth and, summoning up all the determination I could muster, headed once more for those elusive mountains.

* * *

I was on my way home at last. My spirits improved – a lull in the blizzard. An extraordinary day. Hard as I tried, I just could not shift Lucy out of my head. I kept thinking about her, but life must move on, and I felt the draw of Cambridge, my old and familiar way of life, my routines of work and play. However, it must be said I was neither lonely nor depressed and just the thought of the north line and that dear old Hadley Grange, the green GNR locomotive, cheered me up immeasurably. The very notion of being able to cover long distances across the ice plateau in the relative speed and comfort of a train spurred me on, each plodding, hard won footstep, each surmounting of a fresh new obstacle in the landscape, somehow not entirely in vain.

The north railway, dear old Hadley, where are you when I need you most? Come on, old fella, give us one of those hoots of yours. You're out there somewhere, I can sense it. I've escaped that damned awful steel coffin, at least everything else is surely a bonus. And Lucy. Lucy, I knew in my heart, vampire or no, held some inner affection for me also. So there were indeed positives in my life but, as I well knew to my cost, the great ice plateau could be an unforgiving place and brooked absolutely no sentimentality.

Once more, my energies were becoming severely depleted. I was in desperate need of chocolate, a hot meal, a mug of steaming tea. If only I could attain the north line railway station in the next hour, perhaps there would be a cafeteria, a gents', a washroom. I was now bone tired, not able to think or walk straight. 'Hadley,' I gasped, 'where are you when I need you most, old thing?' My eyelids felt heavy and leaden, my face was blasted by wind, whipped particles of ice and snow flurries, a frozen mask of Jack Frost concealing all but my spectacles.

'Where is this station?' I murmured to myself. 'Is there no end in sight to this fearful trek? The wind's livening up, there's a blizzard heading this way, I'm certain of it.'

Then blessed relief, for up ahead through my crinkly iced-up spectacles, I could vaguely see in the near distance the shape of a cloth and pole tent. My prayers, it seemed, had been answered. Companionship, a refreshing mug of steaming tea, some pemmican or soup on offer for a stranded traveller of the plateau. My stomach groaned in anticipation, every fibre of my being longed to settle down inside the tent and rest a while. The tent, even if unmanned, would offer a passable shelter against the worst of the weather.

I approached the snow-blown flaps, aware of a frugal glow within from a cooker. I peeped round a flap and saw a huddle of shadowy shapes, like animals, clustered round a portable stove. My brogues and socks were brittle with ice. My poor feet felt numb and frozen.

'Good to see you, old man, we've been waiting an awful long time ... knew you'd come back this way sooner or later...'

'Come on in,' said Evans, grinning. 'Settle down, old boy.' He shifted over to make some space. My God, these expedition members looked even more shabby than before, their greenish, yellow faces covered by bushy growths of beard, their hair long and untamed.

'I'm on my way to the north line, Captain Scott, I shan't detain you gentlemen very long. I just thought I'd pop over and say "how do?". I'll be on my way, if you've got a bar of chocolate to spare – or a biscuit?'

'Not unless you come inside the tent, Wilkes. The wind chill is intense; you look on your last legs. Captain Oates, boil up our visitor one of your pemmican hashes. Pour out a cup of warming soup. You're frozen to the core. Look, face it, you have no real choice but to lodge with us. You need *fattening up*. We have meagre rations but you are welcome to them. Eat your fill and then you can smoke your pipe.'

'Fattening up,' agreed Oates, chuckling to himself, and bringing to boil a saucepan of smelted water to which he would add pemmican. 'We shouldn't want you to suffer from slow starvation, old boy.'

A grubby hand, the skin in places rubbed off, reached out and seized my wrist. Captain Scott, surprisingly strong considering his depleted constitution, grasped me more forcefully, pulling me against my will further through the tent flaps. The shapes of the haggard bunch of men within shifted forward as if to pounce. Mouthfuls of predatory fangs flashed in that den, gloomily lit by the cooker. Bony and gnarled yellow fingers, the blackened tips and nails hideously malformed by severe frostbite, clawed eagerly at the frozen, stiffened hem of my coat ... and then there sounded a long, glorious hoot of a locomotive whistle. Hadley!

I suddenly found renewed strength and, upon realising my life depended upon quick and decisive action, I struck out with a swipe from the heel of my shoe, striking something crinkly and brittle akin to papier maché covered with a waxy sealant used for skis, and staggered back out into the snow. Even with the strong, biting wind on my face, a layer of flaky snow compounded against the lenses of my spectacles, mostly blinding my vision. I made some headway straight towards the hazy, glowing orb of a round headlamp light.

A hand, friendly this time, I perceived, grasped my arm and a bewigged stout gentleman in shovel hat, naval coat and breeches, wearing a pair of worn-out buckled shoes, steered me forward over the irregular ridges of sastrugi, assisting my passage by offering me his bulb-handled cane for support and to act as a makeshift ski pole.

'Sir John Franklin. I am delighted to make your acquaintance again, Wilkes.' He sighed. 'My ship is beset with ice and I stay put, but we must hurry if you are to catch your train forthwith. Yonder, atop of the iron beast, I see a lighthouse, our veritable signal beacon. Come sir, Crozier and his men are about and the captain is a determined prey seeker who shall show no quarter. The behaviour of ionospheric storms, the aurora and cosmic rays determine this.'

'I can contest to that,' I answered, remembering how, thanks to Lucy's intervention, the ragged bite marks to my neck healed almost at once and the cleansing replenishment of her own blood, that in the nick of time by its refreshing nature rid my system of the fetid claim of blood kinship to that wretched man who had jumped me at the tourist office.

With Sir John's undoubted urgency and guiding influence, we managed to surmount the last of the sastrugi and staggered up some steps and passed through the ticket hall onto the single line platform. At least we were out of the wind.

'Well, Mr Wilkes, our parting of the ways. The ice storm is passed at any rate. Tell me, what do they think of me in England – in Cambridge, say?'

'You're very well thought of in historical terms,' I assured my friend, returning his bulb-headed cane. 'Your reputation is assured. The mystery surrounding your expedition of the *Terror* and *Erebus* remains on school curriculums and is still written about and discussed to this day.'

'Really? Well, I'm glad to hear it. Ah, a toot of a locomotive whistle. Goodbye Mr Wilkes, and God's speed.'

I bid my dear acquaintance Sir John Franklin a fond adieu, thanking him profusely for all his help. The departure board above indicated:

CAMBRIDGE VIA BERING STRAIT AND BAFFIN ISLAND DEPARTS 12.00. BOARDING.

I was delighted to see the green locomotive Hadley Grange was waiting in the platform, hauling a rake of lighted Pullman cars and wagon-lit carriages.

The station itself, although completely made of ice, resembled those along the branch line I invariably encountered when out and around Cambridgeshire. Doors with signs like 'Waiting Room', 'Parcels Office', 'Ladies' and 'Gentlemen'. Although the rooms themselves were visible from without, the verglas intricacy a marvel to behold, they were of solid form and impossible to enter.

The translucent station canopy dripped a glittering array of icicles, the prim window boxes, flower tubs, fire buckets, the cycle rack, porter's trolley, were exact replicas sculpted in ice. Did I slide about on the glassy platform as on a skating rink? No! I did not. Did Hadley Grange, the GNR engine belching smoke from its chimney, creating intense heat from its fire-box, melt any part of the station building? Apparently not, but I confess I was frankly in no position to overly dwell upon such matters, and with good reason, for looking back through the transparent station, I could see clearly out on the plateau, I was not alone.

I was being pursued from the position of the tent. Scott's expedition had somehow utilised a new-fangled motor tractor with caterpillar tracks, whose combustion engine roared and pumped smoke from its exhaust pipe. The machine, to the outside of which some men were recklessly clinging, rose and fell amongst the sastrugi and for a while its mechanical treads made short work of the bumpy terrain. But, as I suspected, in the severe, low temperature reliability proved a problem, and before boarding the train I glimpsed Oates, Evans, Wilson, Bowers and Captain Scott – tenacious vampires all – forced to abandon their snow vehicle when the motor tractor developed engine trouble with a faulty choke.

I had been earlier assured by Sir John Franklin that Scott and his men were more recently inducted vampires, known locally as 'primitives', yet to develop the more sophisticated ability to transmute matter and travel through time and space – as, for instance, I believed Lucy could do.

'Welcome, we leave right now. I have received via the grapevine an urgent telegraphic communication, a warning, Mr Wilkes,' barked out the metallic voice of Hadley from the speaker grille positioned above the smoke-box door. 'A powerful witch is somewhere on the ice plateau. I confess this is quite unparalleled. Have you on your travels perchance had dealings with such people before, sir? I confess they will normally tend to prefer the warmer climes of the southern provinces. A witch up here in the frozen north? Unheard of. Very queer indeed...'

'I realise to whom the warning refers, Hadley. Her name's Maria Stromberg. I'm afraid I evicted her from a golden coach, burnt it to cinders in fact.'

'A golden what?'

'Never mind, old fella, let's head for Cambridge. I'm

beat. We'll have to deal with the witch problem when we come to it.'

'A witch indeed!' chortled Hadley like a grinding lathe. 'I'd like to see her flying on a broomstick in these temperatures, with one of those silly pointy caps and a cloak, her black cat perched on the rear. Down they'd come, hitting the plateau like a lump of lead – clonk!'

'Unfortunately, she breaks the mould. She's not like your normal witch, Hadley.'

Boarding the train, I was instantly part of a warm and cosy environment. It seemed to me a great burden had at last been lifted and, Cambridge-bound, I was filled with a new zest for life. I looked forward to continuing my research at the faculty. My old familiar routine, the … oh, gracious, the memory of dearest Lucy disturbed my innermost contentment. It was true, I *was*, dammit, in love with her and longed with all my heart that she should share this journey of mine. Where was she now, I wondered? Being chased across the plateau by that Baron von Reitz and his cruel and contemptuous wife, I shouldn't wonder. Hadley gave a great blasting basso-hoot of whistle, and the train plunged into polar darkness. The green Hadley Grange GNR engine seemed to me to possess impossibly fast traction and locomotion.

Travelling in my usual wagon-lit, I had the whole carriage to myself: a foldaway sleeping bunk, a modest library of books, a writing desk and chair, a plush and comfortable seat by the window, and a dining table laid with crisp, starched white cloth, glass and silverware as previously. A dumb-waiter should supply all my needs and there was naturally a two-way speaker grille positioned above the serving hatch should I or Hadley wish to communicate to each other.

Before taking my seat and slinging my bowler hat and city brolly in the rack above, through the oblong facing corridor window, which looked directly into the next carriage, I noticed the back of a pretty lady's head, her bonnet and some blonde curly hair pinned up, peeping above the seat rest upon the left-hand row, and wondered who my fellow passenger on the express might be. Travelling to England perhaps… It would be nice to while away an hour or two, chatting to this young lady, but for now I slumped luxuriously back in my own seat, a committed lounger, and glad of it. A good hot meal was in the offing, which I knew would be served presently.

I took out my battered briar-root pipe and lit the bowl with a match. Blowing out a blue wreath of tobacco smoke, I contentedly gazed out of the compartment window, but there was nothing save impenetrable blackness, the little rural ice station now long ago left behind. The darkness of a polar winter encroached on my conscious mind, certainly, but not enough to affect my inner wellbeing or happiness with the certain knowledge that I was travelling home at last to Cambridge. I was on the move, not having to plod wearily through snow and ice, clamber the endless fissures and sastrugi, bearing down on me the always fearful cold, and unbearably strong and chafing winds of the plateau.

However, not able to stem my curiosity for one moment longer, before I sat down to enjoy an excellent roast meal cooked by Hadley, which had recently arrived at the dumb waiter, I peered once more excitedly through the pane of the corridor window, eager to see whether my mysterious female passenger, of the grey bonnet with the purple silk band, was still at her seat. But no, she had departed. No winter bonnet or curly blonde hair to be seen. I thus left it at that and decided I would head to my bunk after consuming the delicious fare.

'Hadley,' I mentioned between mouthfuls and sips of fine wine. 'May I enquire of a fellow passenger, who is the lady in the next carriage, I wonder? Where did she get on?'

'Lady? There is no lady, sir. You are the only person on board this express. Now settle down for your second course of suet pud and custard.'

'But I quite clearly saw a grey bonnet with a silk band.'

'My dear Mr Wilkes, trust me mate, there is no lady, 'atted or otherwise, residin' on the train. You are mistaken. Lor' bless us sir, you was just come orf the plateau after being chased by those awful 'arf-dead creatures. You was dog-tired, allowing for snow blindness else hallucatin'.'

'I did not imagine this woman, Hadley. Look old fella, we go back an awful long way, I know that, but my old brain-box is perfectly capable of registering a female presence, *a woman wearing a hat.* Got that?'

'Of course, I'll re-check the passenger lists, just as you say, Mr Wilkes, but I really think it's a complete waste of time.'

A hot soak in the tub, a shave and change into clean and neatly ironed pyjamas did my morale a power of good after long exposure to the plateau and the considerable difficulties I encountered to reach the railway station. I had not long got into my bunk, snuggling down and, lulled by the motion of the train, was just falling asleep when Hadley's metallic but impassioned voice came grating from the wall speaker through my subconscious, urging me to get up from my bed and walk.

'Mr Wilkes, Mr Wilkes, wake up – WAKE UP! Your "lady in the bonnet", sir. I believe I've traced her now to the luggage van, one of them dizzy members of the fairer sex what goes orf in search of the buffet car h'an' gets lost. She's locked 'erself in, bangin' on the inside of the door she is, h'an' very keen to get out. Would you be a sport an' go an' rescue 'er? Ladies, I ask you, but what can one do? Sorry to disturb you, like.'

'Oh, do leave off, Hadley!' I mumbled, tucking the eiderdown closer around my chin. 'I've only just got into my warm and comfy bunk, I'm just settling in. Won't it wait? I mean, are you certain it's her in there anyway?'

'Now, that's what I'se call a lazybones attitude, Mr Wilkes. You jest keep orn down the corridors until you reach the luggage van. LUGGAGE VAN – got that?'

'All right, Hadley, don't shout so, I'm on my way. Now, where's that dratted slipper? Ah, found you!'

Somewhat tiredly I rumpled up my dark, untidy hair and ventured forth from my compartment, making progress swaying through the empty wagon-lits to the rear of the fast moving train. At least the plush seated carriages were luxuriously carpeted throughout, pleasantly warm and illuminated with shaded lamps.

At last I was plainly faced with a steel door clearly marked 'Luggage Van'. I paused on the footplate to listen.

'Help – H-E-E-E-E-ELP!' a timid little voice called out from behind the door, a voice which I found most appealing, irresistible to my masculine ego. 'Won't someone please help me?'

'Help is at hand,' said I, releasing the automatic lock so it became disengaged.

'I'm trapped, the door is stuck fast or locked or something.'

'It's all right,' I called out, twisting the handle, trying to keep my feet steady in the wake of the rumbling express. 'Be with you in a jiffy. The buffet car is up the other end.'

'Oh, is it?' came the naïve response. 'I was certain Hadley said something about it being down here. I've been banging on the door forever.'

At last the door gave way, and I entered the gloomy luggage van stacked with portmanteaux, travelling trunks and suitcases. My eyes took some time to adjust, to become accustomed to the more spartan surroundings.

I was of course expecting a prim little lady in a bonnet. But I was mistaken. My very worst fears were about to be realised. I was drawn instead into the intimidating presence of an extremely tall and imperious looking, dark-haired woman, clothed from head to toe in black, wearing a long, funereal gown and hood, the expression upon her horsey countenance both cruel and calculating, acutely sharp fangs pinching her lower lip, wholly endemic of her species. She allowed me a chilling smile of recognition before beckoning me to come hither.

I was aware the luggage van door had shut behind me with a definitive clunk and that bolts were slithering across of their own accord.

Beside Irena Reitz, the mistress of Vratnik Castle, was her diminutive husband, the baron, a small-boned, cherubically fair midget with a shock of neatly combed blonde hair and freckled nose. He wore a floppy bow tie, a velvet jacket and pantaloons.

He squealed like an excited rodent and propelled his high chair along on its tiny metal castors like a motor racer, skirting round the bench where a steel coffin lay placed on top, the streamlined lid in closed position, a curtain discreetly drawn across its viewing window.

The baron gazed up at me, evidently with some amusement.

'So, now you have had your little holiday, your vacation,

Herr Wilkes, it is time to return forthwith to the crevasse, your home from home within the ice cavern many hundreds of feet below ground. Your exile continues, yes! Far from being angry at your contemptuous behaviour, Irene and I are most concerned for your welfare and have this time employed a far more advanced design of coffin, impregnable and impossible to escape from.'

'Then you, dear Baron, had better find someone else to fit inside it,' said I, summoning up a vestige of courage. 'Because I can assure you I certainly have no intention of taking up residence. I rather like my wide open spaces and being able to move about freely. One actually prefers it.'

'You must serve your time. I have not forgiven, nor forgotten, the fatal damage caused to my ancestral golden coach, to say nothing of Maria Stromberg's destroyed giant gourd burnt to cinders, not even the precious seed-pods spared. You were the ringleader, oh yes you were, Herr Wilkes, of that insidious mob from The Block and Stake in Karstein. And you're not about to escape summary justice.'

'I mean, it is not as though a coffin is that uncomfortable,' chided his wife, the formidable vampire Irena, her diaphanous facial skin undergoing a profound marbling effect, a hive, an entire multiplicity of interconnected throbbing veins being brought to the surface as she became steadily more peevish and, I sensed, dangerous to humans. 'You insult us by your brevity. Why, there is even a viewing window incorporated, Herr Wilkes. You are a fuss-pot. When the lid is mechanically raised, you will please step inside and lie down. Accept your fate with dignity and good grace, not like a petulant child – so un-English.'

'Never! Go box up one of your grovelling peasants. I am not a resident of Vratnik, nor am I governed by your vested authority. I am a British subject and you would do well to remember that.'

'Ah, still hoping for a lifeline of last resort are we, Herr Wilkes? On this occasion neither your normally dependable British passport nor those most civil and comforting diplomatic corps from your embassy shall be of any use... But you see you're wrong... You will do our bidding. Has no one explained to you that vampires are endowed with phenomenal powers?'

'I have never sought to deny your supernormal status, Herr Baron.'

'I like that word "supernormal" very much. But I like it even more when I am allowed a practical demonstration. By thus concentrating I can impose my authority. We shall brook no further argument or protestations. Once the coffin lid is raised you step inside – understand? Now, I will clarify.'

Lifting his head back, the diminutive baron, unusually small and resembling more a chubby infant than an adult, bore his fangs in a snarl of contempt and, closing his eyes, proceeded to rock back and forth on his high chair, setting the squeaky metal castors rolling accordingly, the membrane of each eyelid radiating a pulsing red glow, which made his countenance all the more freakish.

I instantly felt the effects. A searing pain entered my forehead, and every nerve and fibre of my brain felt as though my head were being torn apart, the top of my skull being cleaved off.

'All right – stop – stop! I'll do as you say,' I yelped, a total coward to extreme bodily discomfort, clutching my poor hurting head and despondently falling to my knees, drained and weak from my ordeal, wishing he'd obliterate me there and then, magic me into the stirring notes of a Beethoven or Mozart piano concerto. Anything but endure a slow and living death in exile, stuck inside that dratted steel coffin.

'At long last, Herr Wilkes, you are being sensible. The first sensible words I have heard you utter during our entire conversation. "I'll do as you say" – most gratifying. Now Irena, if you would be so good as to open the –'

An interruption. My heart rejoiced. An old ally was close by. Everything suddenly altered in an extraordinary way. A climatic change occurred, of immense moment. I was witness to the whole interior of the luggage van undergoing a rapid freezing-over. Because of the intensity of the perishing cold atmosphere, in a matter of seconds frost fronds and solidifying icicles appeared, covering the ribbed roof and walls of the railway wagon, a rime of coruscating ice, advancing swiftly, imposing itself on every surface, including the two vampires, who were entirely taken by surprise and now resembled glassy, upside-down stalagmites. Immobile, and held fast – stuck solid to the floor of the luggage van. The temperature continued to drop away.

During this time, it must be said, I had attained immunity from the fierce cold, for just as the chilly phenomenon took a grip and began to encroach everywhere, I noticed out of the corner of my eye an object familiar to me. Leaning against an insignificant fire bucket was Sir John Franklin's bulb-headed walking cane, the bulbous ivory handle lit up by opalescent, shifting light patterns. I seized the cane before my fingers became frost coated and instantly felt warmth and renewed vitality surge through my being.

But imagine my surprise when, from the top of the bench, I heard the clockwork whirring of a motor and saw the coffin lid yawning open and my hero and saviour Sir John Franklin himself emerge from within. He hopped down onto the ice rink of a floor, none the worse for his horizontal confinement. Sir John smoothed down his rumpled breeches, re-buttoned his threadbare naval tunic and adjusted his rather misshapen shovel hat.

'Out!' he commanded, shoving me forcibly through the door. 'Out, Mr Wilkes. Gad sir, I managed to sneak in here when the Reitzes' backs were turned. Five minutes at most, with this handy crucifix I have secreted on my person. Perhaps twenty before those clever vampires from Vratnik Castle manage to outwit us. Out! I say. Hasten with all your might to the wagon-lit. Then I secure the crucifix to the frosted-up luggage van door and we're away. Hadley *must* forthwith be alerted.'

The genial old explorer, both brave and clever, paused on the footplate between clattering, wobbling carriages.

'Hadley, Sir John here.' The freezing draught as the express tore along the plateau was of no consequence, merely ruffling his wig. 'How, pray, do we uncouple this confounded baggage chariot? We must of necessity put plenty of cosmic time and space between it and us, you follow. Vampires aboard, two of them, and only twenty minutes to defrost.'

'Gord strewth, unwanted luggage to be sure. Leave it to me, sir. There! I've uncoupled as requested. The luggage van is stranded a mile or so up the tracks. Pursuit unlikely. Them bleeders won't want to risk a well h'aimed shower of sparks from me chimney setting 'em alight now, will they?'

Mission accomplished, before leaping off the footplate and returning to the sub-zero realm of his beloved plateau, the gentleman whom Jack Frost himself would have designated his heir apparent and heartily congratulated for his chilly ambience, bid me a fond adieu, wishing me continued luck and a safe journey back to Cambridge.

* * *

I recall the train was rattling along at a pace. I was lounging in my warm compartment watching the world – or at least chunks, masses of glacial ice – go by, a welcome respite from walking, and much less taxing to the spirits than the eternal plod through snow and ice, I might add. When replete from my earlier five course meal, I nodded off and fell into a contented doze. Some time later, I was startled awake by the rustle of voluminous crinoline skirts.

Opening my eyes, I was surprised to find none other than Miss Blaufelt of the principality of Volknik sat directly opposite, her lavender gloves folded neatly across her lap, wearing that same grey bonnet I had observed earlier.

'Herr Wilkes, I trust I did not startle you? We are on our way to Cambridge, I see.'

'We?'

'Exactly so. Do you not recall my earlier suggestion concerning our engagement?'

'I do not wish to become engaged to you, Katrina. The last occasion upon which I kissed you in a friendly way I ended up at Castle Vratnik in a steel coffin. I do not wish for a repeat performance. Do you mind if I smoke?'

'Not at all.'

'Besides, you know my feelings are set on another.'

Striking a match, I lit my pipe, seeking some sense of comfort while savouring the smoke. But in those same smoky wreathes that wafted and curled up and around the compartment, Katrina underwent an alarming change.

Gone was the firm and stable shape of her petite figure and pixie-like features, to be replaced by a chimerical mass of finest spun cobwebs before she vanished altogether and I was left staring at an annoyed-sounding, disembodied voice, dumbly stupefied, my pipe drooping from my mouth.

'You, Herr Wilkes, leave me with no other recourse but to press my suit more earnestly.'

'You – you, Katrina of all the damnedest people are actually Maria the witch, the invisible entity capable of shape-shifting at will! Are you and Katrina the same then?'

'We are, and have been all along. It was my pleasure to first introduce you to my charms on the little forest railway when you entered our principality. Katrina Blaufelt is my fleshly form, and I have observed on many occasions you are actually rather attracted to it.'

'Blithering nonsense,' I replied gruffly. 'It is Lucy whom I have lost my heart to. You, the queen of the gourds, helped put me in a steel coffin. Lucy helped get me out of it. You are in league with that wretched Baron von Reitz at Vratnik Castle.'

A long witch's wand poked out of the nothingness and jabbed me on the nose – which hurt!

'As I see it, there are but two courses open to us. *Two*, you comprehend, Herr Wilkes?'

'And those are?' I enquired anxiously.

'*One* – that by a witch's spell I shall cause this stupid engine Hadley Grange to jump the rails and go hurtling in a mass of propelled tonnage and hissing, bubbling smoke into the deep waters of the Bering Strait, which we fast approach. You die, the locomotive dies! I, of course survive.'

'And number two?'

'A proviso of sorts.'

There was a shimmering in the air, a brief appearance of spidery cobwebs and I found myself once more sat in the compartment with Katrina, although she was still holding the wand. My pipe had, I found, self-ignited so I puffed on it nervously.

'And that proviso is?'

'Herr Wilkes, I propose that we should get married. We would as a couple be more acceptable to your peers at the science faculty, to Cambridge society in general. Correct behaviour is, I know, rigidly adhered to in your part of the world, doing what is proper and correct, 'doing the done thing', as it is in my own principality of Volknik. Your Lucy being a total barbarian and a loutish gangster of the northern ice plains would have absolutely no inkling what I am talking about.'

'Lucy may be a barbarian, but she's a very pretty one. She is athletic, an outdoors kind of girl,' said I, incensed. 'I have seen quite enough of your snakish temperament for the time being, Katrina, your endless shape-shifting personality, with your affiliation to Hallowe'en. You, who are in your own way as ruthless as she is in hers. What right have you, a witch of longstanding, to pontificate?'

'She is a vampire, sir, a *vampire*, another species to you entirely. What madness has infused your being, what future is there for you and her in a university town like Cambridge? I am at least more akin to your own flesh and blood. What would you become, an undead, at night feeding off undergraduates and those local to the place?'

'I might just submit to that, yes Maria – I mean, Katrina. I must tell you frankly, I love Lucy dearly.'

'Love Lucy!' exclaimed a highly hysterical, metallic voice. Hadley Grange was almost shrieking, or was that the sound of urgent braking? 'Gord 'elp us, Mr Wilkes, that dratted, powerful witch means business. She's got us by the scruff of our necks. Do as she says. Marry 'er for Pete's sake, 'ave done with it and save our skins. I can feel my brakes starting to magically wear out and fail as we speak. You don't need remindin' sir, the Bering Strait is awful cold at this time of year, and we're heading hell for leather straight for a ducking – a final ducking!'

'Then, like you, Hadley,' said I with a stubborn resolve born of foolhardiness, 'I am bound for the drink. If I am to drown at the deep end, so be it.'

Marriage to Katrina was out of the question. It was Lucy Eldridge who held sway over my heart and I loved her, vampire or no, and that was that.

'What a pity your locomotive friend is so heavy and won't float, ha ha ha,' laughed the once again disembodied voice. 'You won't be able to scream for my help when you're seventy fathoms down beneath the Bering Strait, Herr Wilkes, ha ha,' was the last I heard from Madam Witch, now completely invisible, no doubt beating a hasty retreat back to the principality of Volknik, while all I could hear was Hadley's screeching, useless brakes and a long, wailing train whistle, the boisterous precursor of doom, gloom and imminent immersion in freezing water.

There was but a dull splosh. Good gracious, I had severely misjudged my aquatic environment for the freezing morass of dark water rapidly engulfed my carriage and soon I, Humphrey Wilkes of Cambridge, was irrevocably turned into nothing more than an oblong block of ice, hopelessly weighted, *a lumpen, uninteresting, anti-climactical, frozen solid mass.*

I plummeted down, deeper and deeper down ... down into the depths of the Bering Straits, the sinking train likened to a rolling snowball, gathering extra layers of ice, becoming more heavy as we went.

* * *

'Can you hear me, Mr Wilkes? Squeeze my finger – ouch! Not that hard. Matron, his eyes are opening, do come and look.'

'Would you believe it? That old bedridden lump is moving at long last. Fetch Professor Canty, nurse. Miss Barnfield, remain. Do keep up your banter, shout in his ear, keep trying.'

'Can you hear me, Mr Wilkes? It is I, Miss Eldridge.'

My eyes opened. I was aware of a plain magnolia-emulsioned ceiling, hooded electric lamps, half-tiled sterile white walls, the smell of antiseptic, a large window looking over Cambridge, an overcast winter's day. It was raining, of course. A familiar figure stooped over me. I shut my eyes once more, but only for a short time. The steel hospital bed remained fairly comfortable, sheets clean and starched.

'Mr Wilkes, it is I, Miss Eldridge, can you hear me?'

'Of course I can blasted hear you! My eardrum will be perforated if you keep shouting like that. Will you marry me, Lucy? I'd be dead chuffed if you accepted.'

'Are you quite well? You have been in a coma for the last month or so, Humphrey, but, bless you, I *shall* accept your proposal.'

'What happened to my Townsend Tourer, Lucy? Is it fixable? We were going for a ride in the country – on the Saturday, wasn't that right?'

'Why yes, our crowd from the faculty were to meet at your house: Mr Clancy and Thompson, and me and Eth. Your bike's a total smash-up.'

'Hang those three, it's us I'm interested in. Change of plan – once I'm up and about and I've got me a new cycle, we shall ride post haste to Simpsons the jewellers along the High.'

'Oh, Humph, to choose an engagement ring? You are a sweetie-pie.'

'A wedding ring, Lucy. No time like the present. We shall get the banns read in church by that padre, old Reverend Ecclestone, or shall we get married in the hospital chapel? I'm game if you are. Now fetch me that dressing gown, will you, there's a good girl? I want to get out of bed and have a toddle around. Yes, and those two rubber-tipped canes. Ah, Sir John Franklin, I knew I should see you again some time.'

'Sir John? No, you are mistaken, Mr Wilkes. I am Sir Alan Canty, your attending surgeon. That's it, nurse, plump up the pillows. You're a bit weak on your feet for tearing around the ward just yet. Best save your strength and those sticks for another day.'

'Yes, I'm still very wobbly, but I'm certain we met before – the ice station, wasn't it?' I queried.

'The iced bath, more like. A radical and innovative treatment. I'm glad the operation proved a success, anyhow! We thought we'd lost you on a number of occasions, Wilkes. You were "touch and go", gravely ill and in a deep state of coma.'

'On the contrary, I was on an amazing journey, Sir Alan – and I'm feeling much better. Thank you for saving my life.'

* * *

A YEAR LATER

On the Monday morning, our lighted bus made its slow, jerky way from the depot up Drummer Street, along rainy Emmanuel, the majority of passengers engrossed in their newspapers, enjoying a pipe or first cigarette of the day, immersing the top deck of the No. 14 in a smoky, nicotine-filled haze.

Staring out of the rain-spotted window, my own pipe alight with the best of them, we of the morning crush inhaled and exhaled tobacco smoke as one mass.

Never without my two-ounce tin of Ogden's Flake secreted in the pocket of my tweed jacket, I puffed away, perusing the morning edition of the *Cambridgeshire Times*, when, glancing up through the dingy murk, the sea of obscuring hats and scarves, I saw a slender figure sat near the front of the bus wearing a grey bonnet, encircled with a silky purple band perched atop a mass of blonde, curly hair. The back view seemed vaguely familiar.

Breathing hard, a moist pebbly sweat surfaced on my brow and, keeping my pipe clenched between my teeth, I nearly chewed a hole in the stem. I made a grab for the backrest of the seat in front, gripping it so tightly my knuckles turned white. I was undergoing what in modern parlance is termed 'a panic attack'.

'It can't be, not her, not here in Cambridge.' My heart was thumping, my mind undergoing a re-run of my epic last calamitous journey with Hadley Grange. Ping, ping, I heard the bell go.

'CAT!' someone, a girl, shouted, which made my skin crawl. 'Cathy, put that gasper out, ours is the next stop. Don't forget your satchel.'

There was a scuffle of movement and for a moment

there I mistook the schoolgirl on the bus wearing her grey uniform bonnet for a manifestation of Katrina Blaufelt. I breathed a sigh of relief, and everything came whirring back into focus. But what this incident did reveal, as I reached for my pair of rubber-tipped canes and joined the throng stampeding down the twisty flight of stairs, wielding their brollies and briefcases, was that a link existed in the subconscious between the actual world I inhabited and the other place I journeyed to when in hospital undergoing complicated cranial surgery and lying in a coma.

A mere frightening coincidence, seeing that dratted grey bonnet, enough to trigger a nasty shock to the system. After all, Katrina was not someone I was particularly keen on meeting again.

That evening, after work, when I had returned home to my three-storeyed terraced house, I kissed my wife Lucy, patted the dog and settled down in my chair before the coal fire to smoke a cigarette. Later, I moseyed into our snug kitchen to soak up the domestic atmosphere. Alloy saucepans wobbling, steaming away on the hobs of the Aga, the smell of meat roasting in the oven, admiring my wife as she laid the table for dinner, pinching her posterior playfully. Lucy said that dinner would be ready in half an hour so I decided to go for a stroll in the garden. I had changed into my old cardigan, galoshes and tweed flat cap.

It was a drizzly night in late October, damp and dreary, no moon or stars to talk of, the ground saturated and wet underfoot. I limped up the path, leaning on my rubber-tipped canes, keeping my bicycle lamp fairly steady, and beyond the gate came to that patch of ground at the back where there was the compost heap, bonfire mound, the shed with the asphalt roof, our gardener's wheelbarrow tipped over on its side ... and a faucet screwed to a metal pole stuck in the ground, at this time of the year the tap so stiff it would be almost impossible to turn. In summer the hosepipe would be attached, and water flowing, but in October I guessed the tap would be rusted solid, clogged up and stuck firm. Shining my lamp around, I noticed our clump of wild, scraggy pumpkins had not come through this year. Perhaps Reg, our gardener, had dug or pulled up the vines and tossed them on the compost.

'Herr Wilkes, Herr Wilkes, come closer, I'm over here.'

I baulked. A feminine voice, foreign and very soft, almost a whisper, but it was real...

'Come closer,' the tiny voice insisted. 'That's it, grab the tap, I'm speaking to you through the nozzle. Twist the tap round as far as it will go. My voice shall be enhanced, Herr Wilkes, the volume increased.'

I turned the faucet full on, but naturally water was not what came out but rather hot air!

'What do you want, Katrina?' I barked. 'I'm just about to have my dinner. Lucy will be expecting me back at the house.'

'How sickeningly domestic you've become, tied to a woman's apron strings. You will be sharing the washing up, I suppose. "I dry, you wash up, darling." How perfectly pathetic. I cringe at the very notion.'

'Lucy and I will be sharing washing up duties,' I confirmed. 'As a married couple we delight in such simple pleasures.'

'Like, "do you want a sherry dear?" Kowtowing to her in your carpet slippers, grovelling with an offering of nuts or cheesy crackers. I feel nauseous at the thought. Your baby is due when?'

'Why do you ask? What business is it of yours? Are

you wearing your pointy hat, Miss Blaufelt? Did you perchance fly here on your broomstick? I think you'd look rather fetching stuck in a shop window in Cambridge this Hallowe'en with a pumpkin jammed in your mouth, or, yes, I know – a mannequin to be set alight on Guy Fawkes' Night by me with a match.'

'That's more like you, Wilkes, angry and sarcastic, hints of witch burnings and All Hallows Nacht. A real Karstein man at last. I asked when your baby is due?'

'I'm not sure, six months, I think.' I was desperate to be rid of Katrina. But how…?

'Soon shall come a craving for lumps of coal, or raw worms or a nice slimy toad stuffed with writhing maggots. I envy her diet. Humphrey, let us be friends, at least you know in your heart, ducky, you love me better than her. Be honest for once.'

'How dare you! Lucy and I are very happy together – and content in our domestic life. I think I feel inclined to turn this tap off right now. I've had just about enough of your sauciness, Katrina.'

'Before you do – get rid of me, I mean – hear me out, Wilkes, for I bring glad tidings. On Christmas Eve, at the height of your quaint Englander churchy, festive month of carols, bells, candles and holly, one of your dearest friends and most beloved of acquaintances will be passing through Cambridge and has let it be known that he will be visiting your "homey" terraced house in Knowle Crescent for a glass of sherry and a little chat. *Two* of your old acquaintances – I stand corrected.'

'Friends? You mean Sharna and Griselda? Whom do you speak of? Dear old Herr Bauer and his wife Netta from the Block and Stake? To be sure, I would offer them a glass of sherry – and our spare room for the night.'

'I mean Baron von Reitz and his sharp-fanged wife, Irena, you simplistic fool. They have apparently some unfinished business to attend to. Ha ha.'

The tap began to squirt copious amounts of foul green sludge, which sprayed all over my trousers, staining them and my woollen cardigan awfully. The unpleasant odour of putrefied slime stayed with me for days. Worse, of course, was the sly way Katrina cleverly instilled fear in my heart. The cruel understanding I might not have escaped Vratnik's summary justice after all.

I turned round in a huff, waving my lamp about, ready to make my way back to the house along the dark and sloshy path. Whatever she had said, I felt more determined than ever to somehow push it all to the back of my mind, to put the whole episode of Katrina's mocking, disembodied voice down to imagination, plain and simple, something sparked off in my brain after seeing that distinctive bonnet again on the bus going to work.

Ready to leave, the beam of my torch dawdled hesitantly on the muddy patch of ground that previously, a few minutes before, had been barren and a mire, but which now, I could not deny, no matter how hard I tried to convince myself otherwise, was home to six big, fattened and ripe pumpkins, healthy and round gourds, weighty and grinning with vitality on the vine, having recently sprung from the earth and flourished.

* * *

The intervening period between the end of October and Christmas week passed uneventfully. I continued to work at the faculty, and on a Wednesday visited my GP, who prescribed powders to help me sleep better (no nightmares to talk of), and during the following week at the hospital, a consultant, Mr Ebury, gave me a thorough examination.

Although I walked with the support of a pair of rubber-tipped canes, my limp was gradually improving. The slight speech impediment remained but we were working on that. No complications had arisen and I had been pain-free for some time, clearly my aftercare not requiring more surgery. Everyone at the department of neurology was pleased for my continued recovery, as indeed was I.

Further along the corridor was the hospital psychologist, dear old Mr Hart, with his dandruffy, salt and pepper hair and shabby black suit, as usual sat on a hardback chair in his cubby hole. Over a cup of tea I answered a few easy, non-probing questions, we smoked our pipes agreeably and made casual conversation. Twenty minutes elapsed and another appointment was booked for February 10th.

I chose naturally not to mention to Mr Hart, or give any credence to, my so-called 'panic attacks' both on the bus and at the end of my garden. The time for that sort of nonsense was over and I needed to get on with real life. Disturbing grey bonnets and talking taps were not going to endear me to anyone of a sane disposition. Lucy was expecting our first child, I had to be aware – not living a half-dream.

Generally, as foggy November passed into freezing December, our little home in Cambridge flourished and we grew more and more fond of each other. Sometimes, smoking my pipe of Ogden's Flake in front of the hearth of an evening, curtains drawn and lamps lit early, I would ponder which was the greater Lucy. The delightful vampire who had pretty well single-handedly got me out of all sorts of tight spots and scrapes, or plain Lucy Wilkes of

Knowle Crescent in Cambridge, now my wife, sat opposite me knitting, who had kept vigil by my bedside during my state of deep coma and, after my awakening, agreed to marry me and had been so influential latterly in aiding my recovery, helping me to walk again without a limp and speak properly without slurring my words. Some achievement, I owed her much.

The day before Christmas Eve, although it was far more likely for the town to be swept by gales and torrential rain, that year it snowed heavily and the whole of Cambridge got a good covering. Pavements, roads, gardens, roofs of houses, Trinity College fountain and university buildings received two or three inches at least and, due to a severe frost that night and a dip in daytime temperatures, although no more snow was forecast, patchy areas in effect hung around, giving us in Knowle Crescent a whitish festive outlook. Even if that meant on Christmas Day itself just a heaping of grubby snow round by the bird table, a lump or two dolloped on the lawn or a dusting on the shed roof, that was better than none at all. The bitter cold temperatures were not to everyone's liking but persisted throughout Christmas.

I recall that night upon the eve of Christmas, Lucy and I had just attended a midnight carol service. We arrived back from church, and writhed out of our woolly gloves, hats, scarves and coats in the hall. Glowing, full of optimism and joy for the future, we waltzed clumsily round our tiny sitting room with its crowded bookshelves, me leaning on a cane and dragging my foot. Our cosy nest felt warm and inviting, a coal fire flickered contentedly in the grate behind the mesh fireguard, the mantelpiece Lucy had sanded and painted magnolia gloss a couple of weeks previously was now decorated with sprigs of holly and crinkly paper bells, the ceiling strung with a colourful variety of home-made paper chains, the loops cut out and gummed by us.

In the corner was our Norwegian spruce from the covered market. Brown paper packages were heaped round the tub, itself wrapped in a single sheet of bright red crepe paper.

Bottles of Harvey's and Croft Original, along with plates of walnuts and tangerines, were placed on an oval table, once belonging to Lucy's grandmother Maud.

The steady heat from our kitchen stove kept the downstairs warm, and paraffin heaters kept us comfortable upstairs despite the bitterly cold night-time temperatures.

Lucy went up to bed, with our dog Beatty at her heels, while I dutifully went into the kitchen to lock up and bolt the back door. My happiness knew no bounds. I visualised us sat in our usual pew at church on Christmas morning, our friends invited back for a convivial sherry, Christmas lunch, Lucy and me tearing open our presents (two for the dog) and kissing beneath the mistletoe.

I had got so carried away with last-minute shopping, gadding about the closed market, present wrapping, spoiling my wife, that I was completely guileless, unaware, unsuspecting of the darker, more sinister undertones waiting patiently for a time and place to strike at their most ferocious.

I leaned down to plump Beatty's tartan blanket in the wicker dog basket and, looking about me one last time, extinguished the lights.

Upon re-entering the sitting room, my entire world crumbled before me and fell away. I was but a tiny, insignificant, disabled worm wriggling helplessly in the tearing, mighty beak of a hungry black crow.

The dreaded squeak of a high chair on castors was all that was needed to give me a sinking feeling in my stomach, a sense of doomed finality, an abrupt curtailment of all that was happy and free and wonderful.

Baron von Reitz, his round, cherubic face glowing in the firelight, occupied one side of the homely hearth and his horse-faced, tall and intimidating vampire of a wife, Irena, the other.

The baron bared his sharp teeth in a feral snarl of utter contempt as I cowered in the corner over by the Christmas tree.

'A very, merry olde Englander Christmas to you, Herr Wilkes. Irena and I wish you continued festive joy, with the proviso that when you are exiled to the Great Plateau this time, you stay there!'

The coal fire reacted by flames bursting up the chimney as though hastily beating a retreat from the pair.

'In effect, Baron, you have somehow, embracing the relativity of time, successfully breached the dimensions between this world and your own. I am astounded, devastated!'

'Thank you for being both so scientific and complimentary, Wilkes. The faucet at the end of your garden informed you of our pending visit, did it not, allowing you plenty of time to prepare, make your last will and testament, tie up any loose financial ends, leaving all your worldly chattels to your spouse.'

Tears began streaming down my cheeks, my spectacles misted over as I experienced such utter dejection and sorrow.

'How cruel you people are!' I commented. '*Cruel, cruel, cruel*, and me with a disability.'

'*Fair*, not cruel,' the baron corrected me, leaning forward in his high chair, his voice rising an octave as he sought to set out the facts as he saw them. 'Go back awhile, Herr Wilkes – you alone led that … that marauding band of drunken riffraff from the Block and Stake in Karstein and, while you yourself were in your cups, wantonly burnt down my engine shed, incinerating the golden pumpkin coach, nearly causing a serious rift to form between us and that clever witch Maria Stromberg. You were not in England, remember, but in the principality of Volknik which, may I remind you, is under our jurisdiction, not your Houses of Parliament or the British government.'

'I understand that, but for pity's sake, Baron, Lucy is expecting our first child. Can't you reconsider? Put my exile off for a few years, wait until my leg gets better?' I confess I was desperate to find some way of gaining clemency.

'The past catches up with one eventually, Herr Wilkes,' he sniggered. 'Now, we shall materialise the steel coffin over by your twinkling tree in the corner and be on our way. Once you are safely contained and secure, the three of us shall depart this night for Vratnik Castle. We wish your festive Christmas decorations a fond farewell – no!'

'One moment, Baron von Reitz.' My dearest Lucy was paused at the foot of the staircase in her white nightgown, so reminiscent of a shroud, cradling Beatty, the dog. She must have overheard all. How like a spectral wraith, her long dark hair parted in a complementary style to Irena's. Without foundation or makeup in the wavering light she seemed pale, tubercular, her lips at the same time sensuous, slightly parted, for could that be the faintest glimpse of fangs I saw or merely the flickering coal fire playing tricks in the grate?

Not surprisingly, the Reitzes warmed to her at once, looking upon her as one of their own, charmed by her deathly, grave, shrouded countenance, her ever so Gothic appearance which, as vampires of long standing, they appreciated.

'I have an alternative solution which may suit both parties. Will you hear me out, Herr Baron?'

'Of course, Mrs Wilkes, but alas, what is there left to negotiate? Precious little, I fear. After all, your husband has absconded once already. Upon this occasion the law of Volknik must and shall be upheld.'

'Let Lucy Wilkes have her say,' insisted Irena while enviously admiring my wife's abundant locks, for Lucy's glossy hair, luxurious and long, hung all the way down from her shoulders to her waist, and was perfectly combed in the style then fashionable with vampires.

Stroking our little pup's broad head energetically, my wife stretched and flattened Beatty's ears, and boldly suggested the following:

'In return for a reduced sentence, I wondered if you, Herr Baron, feudal ruler of the principality of Volknik, and your gracious wife, Irena, would do Humphrey and me the honour of becoming Godparents to our little baby when he or she is born in five months' time or so. And also attend the christening.'

'Lucy!' I exclaimed, flabbergasted. 'Are you mad, have you lost all sense of proportion? A christening takes place in a church.'

'Hold your tongue, husband,' she hissed. 'My apologies, Herr Baron.' Baring her fangs in my direction, drawing back her upper lip in a vile snarl worthy of an aggressive vampire wishing to impose its authority and achieve overriding dominance, Lucy was impressive. Irena, I am sure, approved of my wife's ferocity and Reitz was watching from his high chair with unalloyed delight.

'I realise this may sound presumptuous, but might we even name our child in your honour? If it is a girl, Irena, and if a male…'

The emotional baron, wearing his velvet coat and embroidered frilly collar, wriggled round in his high chair. The bartering for a life by a pretty, determined woman evidently appealed to his judgemental nature, so much so that the vampire's wooden-heeled clogs began clack-clacking excitedly against the legs of his high chair, causing it to roll back and forth on its tiny castors, making the seat dangerously prone to tipping over into the coal fire – which of course, unfortunately, it didn't. He at length folded his chubby hands across his lap and expounded thus:

'Both of us are touched by your offer, Mrs Wilkes, your proposal is significant – *different.* Irena and myself have been married now for many a long century, but never been blessed with children of our own. The idea of becoming a Godparent strikes me as quite novel. What say you, dearest wife?'

'Godparents to a human child,' she answered in a deadpan way. 'Well, there is a first time for everything, I suppose.' As the vampire became more animated the veins in her face throbbed, undulating beneath the surface, repulsively wriggling about like a nest of disturbed grass snakes. 'We should be free to visit our Godchild here in Cambridge, Lucy?'

'You will be henceforth regarded as part of the family, Irena, baby's intimate circle. Of course you and the baron may visit us whenever you choose. Humphrey and I are hardly in a position to impose restrictions anyhow.'

'Quite so, where will this Englisher baptismal ceremony take place?'

'Saint Mark's up the road is a pleasant parish church. We were married there and attend regularly.'

'Tell me, Baron,' I asked incredulously, 'does not the

religious ambience of a church, the prospect of an altar cross and assorted crucifixes put you vampires at risk? At least cause you to become uncomfortable?' I got up unsteadily from behind the Christmas tree, accidentally shaking the branches, causing the gold and silver baubles to twirl about and showers of pine needles to embed themselves in the carpet fibres.

'Really, Wilkes, where do you people pick up all this misinformation about vampires?' said the baron, scratching his domed head in bewilderment. 'I do not happen to shake in my boots whenever I encounter a sprig of garlic flowers, nor do I crumble into dust deposits at the mere sight of a crucifix. We enjoy visiting crypts of old churches, don't we, Irena? In your world, and in ours, pausing to rest our feet and lie down a while in one of those dear old-fashioned, lead-lined coffins, often so dusty and derelict, breathing in the sense of the past. Mind you, there is one defining issue which represents life or death to our kind. I refer, of course, to *daylight.* The Englander christening of our Godchild had better take place after sunset when your Cambridge shire is nice and dark. Does that pose any difficulties?'

'Not at all, Herr Baron, I shall have a word with our vicar about scheduling arrangements. Being Anglicans we are generally fairly flexible when it comes to weddings and christenings and so on. So, we are agreed! Godparents it is then.'

Lucy put down the petrified dog, who scampered off to the kitchen, and rushed across to embrace both Baron von Reitz and his ultra-tall wife in turn.

After this buoyant rush of emotion the baron, whose eyes glowed with a red iridescence, wagged his judicial finger in a desultory way from atop his wheeled high chair and prepared to offer me a short summing up before passing sentence.

'You owe your clever wife much, Herr Wilkes,' said he, haughtily. 'She alone has spared you untold torture, misery and lengthy confinement in the steel coffin. Be grateful that we, the Godparents of your first-born, find her terms for a reduced sentence acceptable and because of this I, the Godfather, impose a fine of one bag of gold coin. Failure to deposit this amount into the coffers of Vratnik Castle will result in my reverting to former sentencing.' He sneered at me and then cast a crafty glance at his wife, whose long, horsey face with its prominent cheekbones, became that much more horrible in the firelight as she waited to see my reaction.

'How long do I have to procure this bag of gold?' I demanded to know.

'Five minutes.'

Still reeling from this utter cruelty – even at this late stage the man was capable of downright nastiness – I looked about me and decided to improvise, snatching a convenient novelty bag of chocolate gold coins from a branch of our Christmas tree and handing them in, hopeful he would not notice the difference. They rattled fairly realistically and I was amazed.

Baron von Reitz, growling under his breath, begrudgingly accepted the payment and pocketed the gold coins forthwith in his velvet jacket.

* * *

It is hard to believe that, as we sat around the fire on Boxing Day, us and the dog, cracking walnuts and peeling tangerines, homely and comfortable in our snug environment, peaking out of the window now and then at the wintry sky, mounds of frozen snow dappled here and there on the lawn, a clump or two round by the bird-table, patches remaining on the shed roof, that this same book-lined enclosed space we now inhabited had upon the eve of Christmas become a courtroom where, for a short while, my very life hung in the balance. Without my wife's 'joke-shop' fangs and her ridiculous proposal for a more lenient sentence, I might well have been spirited away through the dimensions to serve my time on the Great Plateau and worse, darling Lucy may never have seen me ever again here in Cambridge. Well, perhaps knowing her she would have somehow managed to beat a path through time and space and come and rescue me with Sharna and Griselda.

Throughout the year, my hospital visits continued and the consultant, Mr Ebury, was pleased with my continued progress. I no longer require a pair of rubber-tipped canes to get about and have resumed my bicycling, having recently been out and about Cambridge on a shiny, new red and black Townsend Tourer, a gift from Lucy for my birthday. It has the addition of a large and commodious creaky wicker basket attached to the handlebars, ideal for shopping but also for carrying our little baby daughter, Irena, who gurgles and blows saliva bubbles quite contentedly and enjoys the sensation of cycling along at speed and having the sun beating down on her bonneted face.

I had my last appointment with Mr Hart, the hospital psychologist, yesterday. Naturally, no mention whatsoever of my narrow escape from the clutches of Baron von Reitz. For the last few appointments squeezed into his cubbyhole we have smoked our pipes agreeably, chatting about lawn mowers and classical music. Thankfully, the tap at the end of the garden has not started up a conversation either.

The question in any reader's mind consulting this narrative must surely be… Did the Reitzes ever actually attend the baptism of our little girl at Saint Mark's? Yes and no, we still are not entirely sure. Curiously, when we crowded round the font there was a noticeable fragrance of violets. The baron, I recall, favoured violet water cologne. Lucy remarked upon this as well, as did the vicar. But one thing is certain, undeniable, irrefutable: upon returning to our little terrace in Knowle Crescent and coming upstairs to baby's room, there was placed in the bottom of the cot (all of us were witness to this) upon the pink eiderdown, a weeny bracelet that I should judge was of black jet, a product of Whitby, uniquely mined from the cliffs, with tiny jet skulls dangling from it like charms.

Our baby adores this very funereal trinket and refuses, indeed won't tolerate, the alternative fastening of a rival silver christening bracelet purchased from a reputable jeweller along Cambridge High Street by my mother.